# THREE NOVELLAS

Joseph Roth titles
published by The Overlook Press

*The Radetzky March*

*The Emperor's Tomb*

*Tarabas*

*Confession of a Murderer*

*Job*

*Flight Without End*

*The Silent Prophet*

*The Spider's Web* and *Zipper and His Father*

*Hotel Savoy*

*Right and Left*

*Joseph Roth*

# THREE NOVELLAS

Fallmerayer the Stationmaster

The Bust of the Emperor

The Legend of the Holy Drinker

THE OVERLOOK PRESS

New York, NY

This paperback edition first published in the United States in 2003 by
The Overlook Press, Peter Mayer Publishers, Inc.
141 Wooster Street
New York, NY 10012
www.overlookpress.com
For bulk and special sales please contact sales@overlookny.com

Library of Congress Cataloging-in-Publication Data

Roth, Joseph, 1894–1939
[Short stories. English. Selections]
Three novellas / Joseph Roth.
PT2635.O84A24 2003    833'.912—dc21    2003054851

Book design and type formatting by Bernard Schleifer
Manufactured in the United States of America
ISBN 978-1-58567-448-0
3 5 7 9 8 6 4 2

# CONTENTS

# Fallmerayer
# the Stationmaster

TRANSLATED FROM THE GERMAN
BY JOHN HOARE

I

The remarkable destiny of the Austrian stationmaster, Adam Fallmerayer, deserves without a doubt to be recorded and preserved. He lost his life, a life which, incidentally, would never have been brilliant—and perhaps not even satisfying in the long run—in the most bewildering way. Based on all the knowledge which people can have of one another, it would have been impossible to prophesy an unusual destiny for Fallmerayer. And yet it came to him, it seized him, and he even seemed to give himself up to it with a certain pleasure.

He had been a stationmaster since 1908. Soon after taking up his duties at the station at L, on the southern line, barely two hours distant from Vienna, he married the worthy, but somewhat limited and not particularly youthful daughter of a senior chancery official in Brums. It was a "love-match," as it used to be called in those days when "marriages of convenience" were still customary and traditional. His parents were dead. When Fallmerayer married he nonetheless obeyed the very sober dictate of his very sober heart, not the promptings of his common sense. He begot two children, girls and twins. He had expected a son. It was fundamental to his nature to expect a son and to regard the simultaneous arrival of two girls as a painful surprise, if not as a hostile act of God. Since, however, he was secure from material worries and entitled to a pension, he accustomed himself, within a bare three months of the birth, to this bounty of nature, and began to love his children. To love: in other words to care for them with the overwhelming bourgeois conscientiousness of a father and a worthy official.

On a March day of the year 1914 Adam Fallmerayer was sitting, as usual, in his office. The telegraph ticked ceaselessly. Outside it was raining. It was an unseasonably early rain. The previous week they had still had to shovel the snow from the tracks and the trains were arriving and leaving dreadfully behind time. One night, all of a sudden, the rain began. The snow vanished, and opposite the little station, where the unattainable and dazzling splendor of the Alpine snow had seemed to praise the eternal lordship of winter, an indescribable blue-gray haze had for some days past blended clouds, sky, rain and mountain all into one. It rained, and the air was mild. Fallmerayer the stationmaster had never experienced such an early spring. The express trains which were heading south, to Meran, to Trieste and Italy never stopped at his tiny station. The expresses rushed unheedingly past Fallmerayer, who twice daily put on his brilliant scarlet cap and strode onto the platform to salute their passage. They almost degraded him to the level of signalman. The faces of the passengers behind the big windows melted into a gray-white pulp. Fallmerayer the stationmaster had seldom been able to descry the face of a passenger bound for the south, and "the South" meant more to the stationmaster than a mere geographical definition. "The South" was the sea, a sea of sunshine, freedom, happiness.

Certainly, a free railway pass for the whole family's holidays was to be numbered among the rights of senior officials of the southern railway. When the twins had been three years old they had journeyed to Bozen with them. They had taken the slow train for an hour to the station where the proud expresses stopped. They had climbed in, climbed out, and found themselves still a long way from the south. Their leave lasted four weeks. They saw rich people from all over the world and it seemed as though the very ones whom one saw were by coincidence the richest of all. They were not on leave. Their life was one long holiday. As far as one could see—far and wide—the richest people in the world had no twins; particularly not girls. And anyway it was the rich people who really brought "the South" to the south. An official of the southern railway lived permanently in the deep north.

So they traveled back and took up their duties afresh.

Fallmerayer looked up from his desk. It was five in the evening. Although the sun had not set it was dusk already, because of the rain. On the glass canopy of the platform the rain beat as unceasingly as the ticking of the telegraph, and it was a comfortable, uninterrupted dialogue between science and nature. The big, blueish flagstones beneath the platform's canopy were dry. But the tracks—and between the tracks the little stones of the gravel—glistened despite the darkness in the moist magic of the rain.

Although stationmaster Fallmerayer's nature was not

endowed with much fantasy, it nevertheless seemed to him that this day was quite particularly pregnant with Fate, indeed he began to tremble as he looked out of the window. The express to Meran was due in thirty-six minutes. In thirty-six minutes, so it seemed to Fallmerayer, night would be absolute, a night to be feared. Above his office, on the first floor, the twins were running wild, as usual. He could hear the patter of their childish and yet rather brutal footsteps. He opened the window. It was no longer cold. Spring had come down from over the mountains. One could hear the whistle of engines shunting, as one did every day, and the calls of the railwaymen and the dull thudding shock of the coupled wagons. All the same, today the locomotives had a special whistle, or so it seemed to Fallmerayer. He was quite an ordinary person, and nothing seemed odder to him than thinking he detected on this day, among the usual and quite unsurprising noises, the sound of an uncommon destiny. In fact, it was on this day that the terrifying catastrophe happened, as the result of which Adam Fallmerayer's life was to be completely altered.

## II

The express had already been announced as a little late on leaving B. Two minutes before it was due through L it collided, as the result of a set of points being misplaced, with a stationary goods train. The catastrophe was there. Hastily grasping some entirely ineffective lanterns, Fallmerayer the stationmaster ran along the tracks towards the site of the disaster. He had felt the need to grasp some concrete object. It seemed to him out of the question that he should run towards the trouble with empty, as it were weaponless, hands. He ran for ten minutes, coatless, the rain whipping ceaselessly against his neck and shoulders.

By the time he reached the scene of the accident, people had just begun to pull out the dead, the injured and the trapped. It grew darker than ever, as if night itself were hurrying to do justice to the first shock and to increase it. The fire brigade came from the little town with flares which crackled and hissed as they fought to beat off the rain. Thirteen coaches lay splintered on the tracks. They had dragged out the driver and his fireman. They were both dead. Railwaymen, firemen and passengers labored at the wreck with anything they could lay their hands on. The injured cried piteously, the rain poured down, the flares hissed. The stationmaster was freezing in the rain. His teeth chattered. He had the feeling that he should be doing something, like the others, but at the same time he was afraid that they might prevent him from helping because it was possible that he himself might have been responsible for the accident. Now and again one or other of the railwaymen who knew him greeted him fleetingly in the urgency of their duty, and Fallmerayer would attempt tonelessly to say something which might equally easily have been an order or a prayer for forgiveness. But nobody heard him. He had never before felt himself so superfluous on this world. He was just beginning to regret that he himself had not been among the victims, when his eye aimlessly fell on a woman who had just been laid on a stretcher. There she lay, abandoned by her rescuers, her great dark eyes bent on the flares nearest to her, covered to her hips in a silver-gray fur coat, and obviously in no condition to move. The rain fell incessantly on her pale broad face and the light of the flares flickered over her. Her face gleamed, wet and silvery, in the magical interchange of flame and shadow. Her long white hands lay on her coat, motionless also, like two wondrous corpses. It seemed to the stationmaster that this woman on her stretcher was lying in a great white island of peace in the midst of a deafening sea of sound and fury, that she even emanated silence. In fact, it seemed as though all the hurrying, busy people wished to make a detour about the stretcher on which the woman lay. Was she already dead? Fallmerayer the stationmaster slowly approached the stretcher.

The woman was still alive. She had been uninjured. As Fallmerayer bent over her she spoke, before he had asked her a question, almost as if she were rather afraid of his question. There was nothing she needed and she thought she could get to her feet. At worst, she had nearly lost her luggage. She could certainly get up. And she at once made as if to do so. Fallmerayer helped her. He took the fur over his left arm, placed his right arm around her shoulders, waited until she was on her feet, laid the fur over her shoulders and his arm over the fur and so they went, without a word, a little way across the tracks and the rubble into the nearby cottage of a pointsman, up a few steps and into the dry, bright warmth.

"You sit quietly here for a few minutes," said Fallmerayer, "I have work to do out there. I'll be back soon."

At the same instant he knew that he was lying, and probably for the first time in his life. Nevertheless, the lie seemed natural to him. Although at that moment he could have wished nothing better than to stay by the woman, it would have seemed terrible to him that she should regard him as someone useless who had nothing better to do while outside a thousand hands were helping and rescuing. So he went out quickly and found, to his own astonishment, that he now had the strength and courage to help, to rescue, to give an order here and advice there. And although he could only think of the woman in the cottage, as he helped, rescued and worked, and although the idea that he might not see her later was gruesome and frightening, he still stayed and worked at the scene of the catastrophe, out of fear that he might leave much too soon and thus expose his uselessness to strangers. And as they followed him with their eyes and stimulated him to greater effort, so he quickly gained confidence in his word and his good sense and revealed himself to be a nimble, clever and courageous helper.

He therefore worked for something like two hours, constantly thinking of the waiting stranger. When the doctor and the nurses had given the necessary first aid to the injured, Fallmerayer turned back towards the pointsman's cottage. He quickly told the doctor, whom he knew, that over there was yet another casualty of the accident. He studied his battered hands and torn uniform with a certain self-consciousness. He led the doctor into the pointsman's room and greeted the stranger, who did not seem to have moved from her chair, with the cheerful and intimate smile which one reserves for old and close friends after a long separation.

"Examine the lady!" he said to the doctor, and went to the door. He waited outside for a couple of minutes.

The doctor came and said, "A little shock. Nothing more. It would be best if she stayed here. Have you room in your house?"

"Certainly, certainly!" said Fallmerayer. And between them they led the stranger into the station and up the stairs to the stationmaster's living quarters.

"In three or four days she'll be perfectly sound," said the doctor.

At that moment Fallmerayer wished she needed many more days than that.

## III

Fallmerayer turned over his room and his bed to the stranger. The stationmaster's wife shuttled busily between the invalid and the children. Twice a day Fallmerayer looked in himself. Stringent orders were given to the children to keep quiet.

By the following day the traces of the accident had been dragged to one side, the customary inquiry instituted, Fallmerayer interrogated and the guilty pointsman dismissed from service. Twice a day, as before, express trains tore past Fallmerayer at the station.

The evening after the disaster Fallmerayer learnt the stranger's name: she was a Countess Walewska, a Russian from the Kiev area, traveling from Vienna to Meran. Part of her luggage turned up and was brought to her; black and brown leather suitcases. They smelt of *cuir de Russie* and unknown scents. The whole of Fallmerayer's quarters smelt of them.

Now that he had lent his bed he did not sleep in Frau

Fallmerayer's, but down below in his office. This meant he did not sleep at all. He lay awake. Towards nine in the morning he visited the room in which the strange woman lay. He asked if she had slept well, whether she had breakfasted and if she felt well. He would take fresh violets to the vase on the sideboard on which the old ones had stood before, remove the old ones, put the fresh ones into fresh water and then remain standing at the foot of the bed. Before him lay the strange lady, on her pillow, under her bedclothes. He mumbled something inaudible. On the stationmaster's pillow, beneath his bedclothes, lay the strange woman with her big dark eyes and white, strong face, as remote as an alien but sweet landscape. "Do sit down," she said, twice each day. She spoke the hard, alien German of the Russians, in a deep, strange voice. All the splendor of the far off and the unknown was in that voice. Fallmerayer did not sit down.

"Excuse me, but I have a lot to do," said he, turning about and leaving the room.

So it went on for six days. On the seventh the doctor advised her to continue her journey. Her husband was awaiting her in Meran. So she went on her way, leaving behind her in all the rooms, and particularly in Fallmerayer's bed, an inextinguishable trace of *cuir de Russie* and some nameless scent.

## IV

This remarkable scent stayed in the house, and in the memory, not to say the heart of Fallmerayer much longer than did the catastrophe. And during the weeks which followed, during which the boring investigation of more precise facts and more detailed origins of the accident pursued their routine course and Fallmerayer was heard a couple of times, he never stopped thinking of the foreigner and gave almost confused answers to plain questions, as if he had been made deaf by the perfume she had left around him and to him. Had his duties not been comparatively simple and he himself not virtually become over the years an almost mechanical part of the service he could not in all conscience have continued in his duties.

Secretly he hoped that each mail would bring news of the stranger. He had no doubt that she would write once, if only to thank him for his hospitality and as a matter of courtesy. And one day a big dark blue envelope did arrive. The Walewska wrote that she traveled further south with her husband. At the moment she was in Rome. She and her husband wanted to go on to Sicily. The following day an elegant basket of fruit arrived for the twins and a bouquet of very delicate and scented white roses for the stationmaster's wife, from Countess Walewska's husband. It had been a long while, wrote the Countess, before she had found time to thank her kindly hosts, but after her arrival in Meran she had taken some time to recover from her shock and she had needed to convalesce. Fallmerayer carried home the fruit and flowers at once. Although the letter had arrived a day earlier, the stationmaster nonetheless held onto it rather longer. The scent of fruit and roses from the south was strong, but to Fallmerayer it seemed as if the scent of the Countess's letter were even stronger. It was a short letter. Fallmerayer knew it by heart. He knew the exact position of each word. Written with big bold strokes in lilac ink, the letters stood out like a lovely host of slender birds in strange plumage, swooping across a dark blue background. "Anja Walewska," ran the signature. He had long been curious about the stranger's Christian name, as though this name were one of her hidden bodily charms, but he had never dared to ask about it. For a while, now that he did know it, it was as though she had made him a present of a delicious secret. And out of a jealous wish to keep it for himself alone he only made up his mind two days later to show it to his wife. From the moment that he knew the Walewska's Christian name he became aware that his wife's name—she was called Klara—was not beautiful. As he saw with what indifferent hands Frau Klara unfolded the stranger's letter, the hands of the foreigner came back to his mind, just as he had first seen them on her furs; motionless hands, two gleaming, silvery hands. I should have kissed them then, he thought for a moment.

"A very nice letter," said his wife and put the letter aside. Her eyes were steel blue, conscientious and not in the least concerned. Frau Klara Fallmerayer had the ability even to raise worries to the level of duties and to derive satisfaction from feeling concerned. It seemed to Fallmerayer, to whom ideas and insights of this sort had always been alien, that he was suddenly aware of this. And that night he gave as a pretext some urgent official duty in order to avoid the room they shared and to lie down to sleep in his office, where he tried to persuade himself that the foreigner was still sleeping above him, in his own bed.

Days went by, and months. Two picture postcards flew in from Sicily, with fleeting messages. Summer, a hot summer, arrived. As the time of his leave approached, Fallmerayer decided not to go anywhere. He sent his wife and children to the mountains in Austria. He stayed behind and continued to attend to his duties. For the first time since his marriage he was separated from his wife. In the quiet of his heart he had promised himself much too much from this solitude. Only when he found himself alone did he begin to realize that he had no wish whatever to be alone. He rummaged in all the drawers; he was looking for the stranger's letter. But he could no longer find it. Frau Fallmerayer had perhaps destroyed it long before.

His wife and children returned, July drew to a close.

Then came general mobilization.

## V

Fallmerayer was an ensign in the reserve of the twenty-first battalion of Jäger. As he occupied a relatively responsible post it would have been possible for him, as for a number of his colleagues, to have remained for a time at home. Fallmerayer alone put on his uniform, packed his kit, embraced his children, kissed his wife and rejoined his regiment. He turned his duties over to his deputy. Frau Fallmerayer wept; the twins were jubilant to see their father in a different uniform. Frau Fallmerayer did not fail to be proud of her husband, but only at the moment of departure. She dammed her tears. Her blue eyes were full of the bitter consciousness of her duty.

As far as the stationmaster was concerned, it was only when he found himself in a compartment with a few comrades that he first appreciated the grimness of this hour of decision. In spite of which it seemed to him that a quite unreasonable gaiety set him apart from all the other officers in the compartment. They were officers on the reserve. Each of them had left a home he loved. And each of them at this moment was a keen soldier. Each of them at the same time was a desolate father, a desolate son. To Fallmerayer alone it seemed as if the war had freed him from a situation with no prospects. Assuredly, he was sorry for the twins. Also for his wife. Certainly, for his wife, too. But whilst his companions, if they began to speak of home, would by look and gesture reveal all the warmth and tenderness of which they were capable, it seemed to Fallmerayer that in order to emulate them, once he began speaking of his own family, he must put even more gloom into his voice and aspect. In fact he would much sooner have talked to his comrades about the Countess Walewska than about his own home.

He forced himself to silence. And it came to him that he was a double liar: first, because he withheld what was nearest his heart; second because now and again he spoke of his wife and children, from whom at that moment he was further removed than from the Countess Walewska, a woman from an enemy country. He began slightly to despise himself.

## VI

He reported. He went to the front. He fought. He was a brave soldier. He sent the customary hearty letters home on service letterforms. He was decorated and promoted to lieutenant.

He was wounded and sent to hospital. He was entitled to leave, which he declined, and returned to the front. He was fighting in the east.

In his time off between actions, inspections and assaults he began to learn Russian out of books which came his way by chance. Almost lustfully. In the midst of stinking gas and the smell of blood, in rain, in morasses of mud, amidst the sweat of the living and the miasma of the decomposing dead, Fallmerayer pursued the alien whiff of *cuir de Russie* and the nameless scent of the woman who had once lain in his bed, upon his pillow, under his bedclothes. He learned this woman's mother tongue and imagined that he spoke with her in her own language. He learned terms of endearment, inflections of meaning, subtle Russian hints of affection. He would talk to her. Separated from her by the whole of a great world war, he would still talk to her. He conversed with Russian prisoners of war. He tuned his ear a hundredfold, marked the most delicate of intonations and copied them fluently. With every new inflection of this alien tongue he drew nearer to the stranger. He knew nothing more of her than what he had last seen: a fleeting word and a fleeting signature on a banal picture postcard. But he lived for her, waited for her and intended soon to speak with her. Because he spoke Russian, and because his battalion was drafted away to the southern front, he was transferred to one of the regiments which, a little later, were incorporated into the so-called Army of Occupation. Fallmerayer was first posted to Divisional Headquarters as interpreter, and subsequently to the "Information and Intelligence Bureau." His final destination proved to be in the Kiev area.

## VII

The name Solowienki he had indeed remembered, and more than remembered, for it had become familiar and native to him.

It was very simple to discover the name of the estate which belonged to the Walewski family. Solowki was its name and it lay three versts to the south of Kiev. Fallmerayer was stricken by a sweetly oppressive and painful excitement. He had a feeling of infinite gratitude towards Fate which had guided him through war to this destination, and at the same time a nameless fear of all that it was now preparing for him. War, going over the top, being wounded, the nearness of death; all these were quite shadowy events compared with what now faced him. All that had befallen him had merely been a preparation—perhaps an unavailing one, who knows—for his meeting with the woman. Was he truly armed against all eventualities? Was she in fact in her house? Had the advance of an enemy not driven her to a place of greater safety? And if she were living at home, would her husband be with her? At all costs he had to go there and see.

Fallmerayer had the horses harnessed and drove off.

It was a fairly early morning in May. The light, little two-wheeled waggonette drove past flowering meadows along a winding, sandy country road through an almost deserted neighborhood. Soldiers marched clattering and rattling along it on their way to their usual training exercises. Hidden in the bright, high, blue vault of the sky, larks were trilling. The thick, dark, belts of little pinewoods alternated with the bright and merry silver of the birches. The morning breeze brought from a great distance broken snatches of soldiers' songs from outlying encampments. Fallmerayer thought of his childhood and of the countryside of his own home. He had been born and raised not far from the railway station for which at the outbreak of war he had been responsible. His father, too, had been an employee of the railway, a minor employee, a storekeeper. Fallmerayer's whole childhood, just like his later life, had been filled with the sounds and smells of the railway, as of the sounds and scents of nature. The locomotives whistled and he held duets with the jubilation of the birds. The heavy smoke of the brown coal settled over the scent of the flowering meadows. The smoky gray of the tracks blended with the blue haze over the mountains to form a mist of nostalgia and longing.

Things were very different here, at once gay and melancholy. No friendly farms here, perched on gentle falls of land, few lilacs to be seen, no saxifrage nor pennywort nor coriander behind fresh painted fences. Only squat huts with wide, deep roofs of thatch resembling cowls, tiny villages lost in the immense landscape and almost invisible even on these plains. How different countries were! Was it also true of the human heart? Will she be able to understand me, Fallmerayer asked himself, will she be able to understand me? And the nearer he came to the Walewski estate, the more fiercely burned this question in his heart. The nearer he came, the more certain he grew that the woman was at home. Soon he had no doubt that he was only separated from her by a matter of minutes. Yes, she was at home.

At the very beginning of the sparse avenue of birches which marked the gently rising approach to the main house, Fallmerayer jumped down. He walked up the drive so as to spin out a little more time. An old gardener asked him what he required. Fallmerayer replied that he wished to see the Countess. He would announce him, said the man, went slowly away and soon returned. Yes, the Countess was there and awaited his call.

The Countess Walewska quite understandably did not recognize Fallmerayer. She took him for another of the many military visitors whom she had had to receive recently. She invited him to sit down. Her voice was deep, dark and foreign. It was familiar and frightening at the same time. But even his fear, even the shiver, were dear to him, welcome, warmly welcome to him after unthinkable years of longing.

"My name is Fallmerayer," said the officer, "and you will naturally have forgotten the name." He began again, "You may recall it. I am the stationmaster at L."

She came over to him and grasped his hand. He smelt again the scent which for countless years had pursued him, which had surrounded, enclosed, tortured and consoled him. Her hands rested for a moment in his.

"Oh tell me, tell me!" cried the Walewska. He told her briefly how it had been with him.

"And your wife and children?" asked the Countess.

"I've not seen them again," said Fallmerayer, "I've never taken leave."

Whereupon a short silence ensued. They looked at one another. The young forenoon sun lay sleek and golden across the room which was broad and low-ceilinged, whitewashed and almost severe. Fallmerayer looked quietly at the Countess's broad pale face. Perhaps she understood him. She rose and picked a gardenia from the middle window of three.

"Too light?" she asked.

"I prefer them dark," said Fallmerayer.

She went back to the little table and rang a small bell. An old servant appeared. She ordered tea. The silence between them did not relent; it grew, rather, until the tea was brought in. Fallmerayer smoked. As she poured his tea he asked suddenly, "Where is your husband?"

"At the front, of course," she replied. "I have heard nothing more from him for three months. We can't even correspond now."

"Are you very worried?" asked Fallmerayer.

"Certainly," she replied, "and no less than your wife probably is about you."

"Forgive me, you are right. That was really stupid of me," said Fallmerayer. He stared into his teacup.

She had debated with herself, continued the Countess, whether to leave the house. Others had fled. She would not run, either from her peasants or from the enemy. She lived here with four servants, two saddle horses and a dog. She buried her money and her jewels. For a long time she searched for a word. She did not know the word for "buried" in German, and pointed towards the ground. Fallmerayer said the Russian word.

"You speak Russian?" she asked.

"Yes. I learned it. I learned it at the front." He went on in Russian and added, "I learned it on your account, for you. I learned Russian so that someday I could speak to you."

She assured him that he spoke admirably, as if he had only uttered that pregnant sentence in order to indicate his ability as a linguist. In this way she deflected his avowal into an insignificant exercise in style.

"Now I must go," he thought. He stood up at once and without awaiting her permission, and knowing full well that she would interpret his discourtesy correctly, he said, "I will come back before long!" She made no reply. He kissed her hand and left.

## VIII

He left, and never doubted that his destiny was beginning to fulfill itself. It is a law, he said to himself. It is impossible for one human being to be so irresistibly driven towards another, and then for the other to remain barred against him. She feels what I feel. If she does not love me now, love me she will.

Fallmerayer carried out his duties with his unfailingly sure reliability as an officer and an administrator. He decided provisionally to take a fortnight's leave, for the first time since he had reported for duty. His promotion to *Oberleutnant* was due within a matter of days. He wanted to wait for that.

Two days later he drove to Solowki. He was told that the Countess Walewska was not at home, that she was not expected before noon.

"Well, then," said he, "I'll just wait in the garden."

And since no one dared to tell him to go, they left him in the garden at the back of the house. He looked up to the double row of windows. He sensed that the Countess was inside the house and had issued orders that she would not receive visitors. In fact he thought he saw the shimmer of a pale dress, first at one window, then at another. He waited patiently and was quite relaxed.

As it struck noon from the church tower he entered the house again. The Walewska was there. She was just coming downstairs in a narrow, black, high-necked dress, with a thin necklace of little pearls around her neck and a silver bracelet at her tight left sleeve. It seemed to Fallmerayer that she had put on armor because of him, and it seemed as though the fire which burned constantly for her in his heart had now borne another strange little blaze. Love was lighting fresh candles. Fallmerayer smiled.

"I've had a long wait," he said, "but I was glad to wait, as you know. I looked up at your windows from the garden and pretended to myself that I was lucky enough to glimpse you. And so I passed the time."

The Countess asked if he would care to lunch, since it was just the right hour. Gladly, said he, since he was hungry, but of the three courses which were then served he only ate ridiculously small helpings.

The Countess told him about the outbreak of war, and how they had returned home post haste from Cairo. She told him about her husband's regiment of Guards; about his comrades; after that, about her youth. It was as if she were searching desperately for stories, as if she were even ready to invent them—anything so as to prevent the silent Fallmerayer from speaking. He stroked his little fair mustache and seemed to listen attentively to everything. He was, however, listening much more attentively to the scent which emanated from the woman than to the stories which she told. His pores were listening. And in any case even her words were scented, and her language. He sensed, anyway, everything she could tell him. Nothing about her could remain hidden from him. What could she hide from him? Her formal dress hid nothing of her body from the knowledge of his eyes. He felt the desire of his hands for her, the desire of his hands for the woman. As they rose he said that he thought he would stay a little. He had leave today and was taking a much longer leave in a few days' time, when his promotion to *Oberleutnant* came through. Where did he think of going, asked the Countess.

"Nowhere!" said he. "I should like to stay with you."

She invited him to stay as long as he liked, that day and later. But now she had to leave him and see to a few things about the house. Should he wish to come there were ample rooms in the house, quite enough for them to have no need of disturbing one another.

He took his leave. Since she could not stay with him, he said, he preferred to go back into the town.

As he climbed into the waggonette she waited on the threshold in her strict black dress, her face broad and white, and as he took up his whip she gently raised her hand halfway in a greeting that was at the same time determinedly restrained.

## IX

Roughly a week after this visit the newly promoted *Oberleutnant* Adam Fallmerayer was granted his leave. He told all his comrades that he intended to go home. Instead he took himself to the family home of the Walewskis, moved into a room on the ground floor, which had been prepared for him, eating every day with the lady of the house, and discussing this and that, things far and near, with her, told her about the front and paid no attention to the content of his stories, let her tell him stories and never listened to her. At night he did not sleep, could no more sleep than he could at home in the station building, years before, during the six days which the Countess had spent over his head, in his room. Now, too, he was aware of her at night above him, over his head, over his heart.

One night—it was sultry and a good soft rain was falling —Fallmerayer got up, dressed and went out in front of the house. Above the wide well of the staircase burned a yellow petroleum lantern. The house was still, the night was still, the rain was still, as though falling on fine sand, and its monotonous murmur was the voice of night's very silence. All at once a stair creaked. Fallmerayer heard it although he was standing outside the door. He looked round. He had left the heavy door open, and he saw Countess Walewska coming down the stairway. She was fully clad, as by day. He bowed and said nothing. She approached him. And there they stood, in silence, for a moment or two. Fallmerayer could hear his heart beating, and it seemed to him as though the woman's heart were beating as loudly as his own, and in time with it. The air seemed suddenly oppressive, not a breath drew through the open door. Fallmerayer said, "Let's walk in the rain, I'll fetch you my coat." And without waiting for her to agree he rushed into his room, came back with the coat, slipped it across the woman's shoulders and then put his arm over the coat, just as he had done with her furs, that time, that never-to-be-forgotten evening of the disaster. And so they went out into the night and the rain.

They walked along the drive. In spite of the damp and the dark, the sparse, slender trunks of the trees shone silvery, as if lighted from within. And as if the silver gleam of these, the most delicate trees in the world had awoken Fallmerayer's heart to tenderness, he drew his arm closer about the woman's shoulder and sensed through the hard, damp material of the coat the yielding richness of her body. For a while it seemed to him that the woman leaned towards him, indeed that she pressed herself against him and yet, barely a moment later there was a clear distance between their bodies. His hand left her shoulders, felt its way upwards to her damp hair, crossed her damp ear and face. Next moment they both stopped, as one, turned towards each other and embraced. The coat slipped from her shoulders and fell to the ground with a heavy thud. Thus, in the rain and the dark, they came face to face, mouth to mouth, and kissed each other for a long time.

## X

At one time Fallmerayer was to have been transferred to Schmerinka, but by great efforts he succeeded in staying where he was. Every morning and every evening he blessed the Army and the Occupation. He feared nothing so much as sudden peace. As far as he was concerned, Count Walewski was long dead, killed in action or murdered by mutinous communist soldiers. The war must go on for ever, and so must Fallmerayer's service, in this place, in this posting. Nevermore peace on earth.

Fallmerayer had unconsciously been lulled into overconfidence, as can happen to many people whose overwhelming passion blinds their senses, robs them of perception and corrupts their intelligence. To him it seemed that no one existed on earth but him and the object of his passion. Obviously enough, however, the mighty destinies of the world proceeded without heeding him. The revolution came. To Fallmerayer, *Oberleutnant* and lover, this was entirely unexpected.

In spite of this, as often happens in moments of acute danger, the mortal blow struck by this fateful hour sharpened even his drowsy wits, and he quickly realized and became doubly aware that it was a question of saving his own life, that of his beloved woman's and above all of rescuing their common valuables. The general confusion into which these sudden events had thrown everything had still left him, thanks to his rank and special duties, access to enough material and armament; he hastened to make immediate use of them. And so during that first couple of days, when the Austrian army was collapsing, the Germans were pulling out of the Ukraine, the Red Russians were beginning their advance and the newly risen peasants were attacking the houses of their previous overlords by fire and plunder, he succeeded in placing at his disposal two well-guarded cars belonging to Countess Walewska, along with half a dozen trusty soldiers with arms and ammunition and enough provisions for a week.

One evening—the Countess was still hesitating to leave

her house—Fallmerayer appeared with a truck and his soldiers and with strong language and almost by main force
compelled his mistress to dig up the treasure which she had
buried in the garden and prepare for her departure. This took
a whole night. As the dim, dank light of the late autumn
morning began to grow they were ready and their flight
could begin.

The soldiers were in the larger of the two cars, which had
a canvas roof. An army driver was in charge of the private car
which followed the first one and in which sat the Countess
and Fallmerayer. They decided not to head westwards, as
everyone else was doing at the time, but to make for the
south. It was safe to assume that every road in the country
leading westwards would be jammed by retreating troops.
And who was to know what to expect at the frontiers of
these newly created states? It was still possible—and this
turned out later to be the case—that fresh hostilities had broken out on the western borders of the Russian Empire.
Besides which Countess Walewska had wealthy and powerful
relations in the Crimea and in the Caucasus. Even in these
changed conditions help was to be expected from them,
should it prove necessary. What was important was a sharp
instinct in both the lovers that at a time when Chaos itself
ruled the whole earth, the eternal sea must offer the only
freedom. The sea, above all, must be their very first destination. To each of the men who were to escort them to the
Caucasus they promised a sizeable sum in pure gold. And so
they drove on in high spirits, and a not unnatural mood of
excitement.

Since Fallmerayer had organized everything very well,

down to every possible and improbable contingency, they succeeded in reaching Tiflis in a very short time—four days in all. Here they released the escort, paid them the agreed reward and just kept on the driver as far as Baku. Many other Russians from noble or upper middle class families had also taken refuge in the south and in the Crimea. In spite of their original intentions they avoided meeting relatives and being seen by acquaintances. Fallmerayer was much more occupied in finding a ship which would take him and his mistress clear out of Baku and into harbor in some less perilous country. In the process it was inevitable that they should meet other families, more or less acquainted with the Walewskis who, like Fallmerayer, had hopes of finding a ship to save them. Inevitable, too, that the Countess should have to lie about Fallmerayer's identity and her relationship to him. In the end it became clear that to achieve the kind of escape they aimed at, it would be necessary to make common cause with other people. They therefore joined up with eight others who wished to leave Russia by sea, finally found a trustworthy captain with a somewhat decrepit looking ship, and sailed to Constantinople, from which city vessels were still sailing regularly to France and Italy.

Three weeks later, Fallmerayer and his beloved mistress reached Monte Carlo, where the Walewskis had bought a little villa before the war. At this moment Fallmerayer felt himself to be at the zenith of his life and happiness. He was loved by the most beautiful woman in the world. Furthermore, he loved the most beautiful woman in the world. Where for long years the powerful remembrance of her had lived in his memory, now she herself stood constantly at his side. From her he derived his life. At every hour he saw himself reflected in her eyes when he was near her, and there was hardly an hour of the day when they were not near one another. This woman, who, such a short time before, had been too proud to obey the desires of her heart and her senses was now blindly and willingly given over to Fallmerayer's passion, to Fallmerayer, a stationmaster on the Austrian southern railway. She was his child, his mistress, his world. Countess Walewska was as happy as Fallmerayer. The tempest of love which had begun to grow in Fallmerayer's heart since that fateful night at the station of L, carried the woman with it, dragged her away, removed her a thousand miles from her origins, from her customs and from the reality in which she had lived. She had been borne away into an utterly alien land of thoughts and sensations. And this land had become her home.

What happened in the great unheeding world was no concern of either of them. The treasure which they had brought with them ensured a life of leisure for several years to come. In any case they took no thought for the future. When they visited the gambling rooms it was from excess of high spirits. They could afford to lose money, and lose money they did, as if to justify the old saying: lucky in love, unlucky at cards. Every time they lost they were enchanted, as if they needed the superstition to be sure of their love. But like all happy people, they were inclined to put their love to the test, and when it survived it, to make their happiness still greater.

## XI

Even though the Countess Walewska had her Fallmerayer all to herself she was nonetheless incapable of going on living—few women can—without the fear that she would lose the man who had inflamed her love and passion. Therefore, although Fallmerayer had given her no cause to do so, she one day began to demand that he divorce his wife and give up his children and his service. Adam Fallmerayer wrote at once to his cousin Heinrich, who occupied a high position in Vienna at the Ministry of Education, and told him that he had abandoned his former life once for all. Since, however, he did not wish to come to Vienna he would prefer that a competent lawyer take charge of the divorce.

A remarkable chance—thus wrote his cousin Heinrich some days later—had led to the fact that Fallmerayer had already been posted missing some two years previously. Since, in addition, he had given no sign of life, he had already been consigned to the ranks of the dead by his wife and his few blood relations. For a long time a new stationmaster had been in charge of the station at L. A long time ago Frau Fallmerayer had gone with the twins to live with her parents in Brums. The best thing to do would be to continue keeping quiet, always provided that Fallmerayer did not experience any difficulties with Austria's representatives abroad in the matter of a passport or anything similar.

Fallmerayer thanked his cousin, promised in future only to write to him, asked him for his silence and showed this exchange of letters to his mistress. Her mind was put at rest. She no longer trembled for Fallmerayer. Only, once infected by this mysterious anxiety, which Nature plants in the souls of women as deeply in love as she was, (perhaps, who knows, in order to ensure the survival of the world), the Countess Walewska demanded a child by her lover, and from the moment at which this desire arose in her she began to give herself up to imagining the outstanding qualities of the child; even, up to a point, dedicating herself to serve it unswervingly. Unthinking, careless, carefree as she was, she nonetheless recognized in the lover, whose boundless love had first aroused her lovely, natural and uninhibited disposition, an example of sensible reflective man. Nothing seemed to her so important as to bring into the world a child which would combine her own qualities with the incomparable qualities of the man she loved.

She became pregnant. Fallmerayer, grateful, as are all men in love, to their fate, as to the woman who has helped them fulfill it, was beyond himself with joy. His tenderness knew no bounds. He saw both his love and his own personality irrevocably confirmed. Now, for the first time, he was fulfilled. Life was yet to begin. The child was expected in six months. Only then would life begin.

Meanwhile Fallmerayer had reached the age of forty-five.

## XII

One day a stranger appeared at the Walewskis' villa, a Caucasian called Kirdza-Schwili, who informed the Countess

Walewska that thanks to a fortunate destiny and thanks, probably, to a particularly venerable portrait, dedicated in the
monastery of Pokroschnie to the blessed Procopius, the
Count Walewski had escaped both the hardships of the war
and the Bolsheviks, and was now on his way to Monte Carlo.
He was to be expected in about a fortnight. He, the messen-
ger, formerly the *Ataman* Kirdza-Schwili, was on his way to
Belgrade in the service of the Tsarist counter-revolution. He
had now carried out his duty. He wished to proceed.

Countess Walewska introduced Fallmerayer as the faithful
*régisseur* of her household. While the Caucasian was there
Fallmerayer kept silence. He accompanied the guest part of
the way. On his way back he felt for the first time in his life
a sharp, sudden pain in his chest.

His mistress was sitting by the window, reading.

"You can't receive him," said Fallmerayer, "let's run for it."

"I shall tell him the whole truth," she replied. "We shall
wait."

"You are carrying my child!" said Fallmerayer. "It's an
impossible situation."

"You're staying here until he comes! I know him! He will
understand everything!" replied the woman.

From then on they did not discuss Count Walewski again.
They waited.

They waited until, one day, a telegram arrived from him.
One evening he arrived. They both fetched him from the
station.

Two guards lifted him down out of the coach and a porter
brought along a wheelchair. They placed him in the wheelchair. He held his yellow, bony, tight-drawn face up to his

wife. She bent down to him and kissed him. With his long, blue, icy, bony hands he kept trying unsuccessfully to pull up two brown rugs over his knees. Fallmerayer helped him.

Fallmerayer saw the Count's face; a longish, yellow, bony face with a sharp nose, light eyes and a narrow mouth, over which grew a drooping black mustache. They rolled the Count along the platform like one of the many pieces of luggage. His wife walked behind the wheelchair, Fallmerayer walked ahead. Fallmerayer and the chauffeur had to lift him into the car. The wheelchair was stowed on top of it.

He had to be carried into the villa. Fallmerayer took him by the head and shoulders, the servant by his feet.

"I'm hungry," said Count Walewski.

As the table was set, it turned out that Count Walewski was unable to feed himself. His wife had to feed him. And as, after a gruesome and silent meal, the time came for sleep, the Count said, "I'm sleepy. Put me to bed."

Countess Walewska, the servant and Fallmerayer carried the Count to his room on the first floor, where his bed was prepared for him.

"Goodnight!" said Fallmerayer. He waited long enough to see his mistress setting the pillows to rights, and how she seated herself on the edge of the bed.

## XIII

At this juncture Fallmerayer left; he was never heard of again.

# The Bust of the Emperor

TRANSLATED FROM THE GERMAN
BY JOHN HOARE

In what used to be Eastern Galicia, and today is Poland, far indeed from the solitary railway line which links Przemysl with Brody, lies the small village of Lopatyny, about which I intend to tell a remarkable tale.

Will readers be so kind as to forgive the narrator for prefacing the facts which he has to impart by a historico-political explanation. The unnatural moods which world history has recently exhibited compel him to this explanation, since younger readers may wish, perhaps need, to have it pointed out to them that a part of the eastern territories, which today belong to the Polish Republic, formed a part of the many Crown Lands of the old Austro-Hungarian monarchy until the end of the Great War which is now called the World War.

Thus, in the village of Lopatyny, there lived the Count Franz Xaver Morstin, the scion of an old Polish family, a family which (in parenthesis) originated in Italy and came to Poland in the sixteenth century. Count Morstin had, in his youth, served in the Ninth Dragoons. He thought of himself neither as a Polish aristocrat nor as an aristocrat of Italian origin. No: like so many of his peers in the former Crown Lands of the Austro-Hungarian monarchy, he was one of the noblest and purest sort of Austrian, plain and simple. That is, a man above nationality, and therefore of true nobility. Had anyone asked him, for example—but to whom would such a senseless question have occurred?—to which "nationality" or race he felt he belonged, the Count would have felt rather bewildered, baffled even, by his questioner, and probably bored and somewhat indignant. And on what indications might he have based his membership of this or that race? He spoke almost all European languages equally well, he was at home in almost all the countries of Europe. His friends and relations were scattered about the wide colorful world. Indeed the Imperial and Royal monarchy was itself a microcosm of this colorful world, and for this reason the Count's only home. One of his brothers-in-law was District Commandant in Sarajevo, another was Counselor to the Governor in Prague; one of his brothers was serving as an *Oberleutnant* of artillery in Bosnia, one of his cousins was Counselor of Embassy in Paris, another was a landowner in the Hungarian Banat, a third was in the Italian diplomatic service and a fourth, from sheer love of the Far East, had for years lived in Peking.

From time to time it was Franz Xaver's custom to visit his relations; more frequently, of course, those who lived within the monarchy. They were, as he used to say, his "tours of inspection." These tours were not only mindful of his relatives, but also of his friends, certain former pupils at the *Theresianische Akademie* who lived in Vienna. Here Count Morstin would settle twice a year, winter and summer (for a fortnight or longer).

As he traveled backwards and forwards and through the center of his many-faceted fatherland he would derive a quite particular pleasure from certain distinguishing marks which were to be picked out, unvarying but gay, on all the railway stations, kiosks, public buildings, schools and churches of the old Crown Lands throughout the Empire. Everywhere the gendarmes wore the same cap with a feather or the same mud-colored helmet with a golden knob and the gleaming double eagle of the Habsburgs; everywhere the doors of the Imperial tobacco monopoly's shops were painted with black and yellow diagonal Stripes; in every part of the country the revenue officers carried the same green (almost flowering) pommels above their naked swords; in every garrison town one saw the same blue uniform blouses and black formal trousers of the infantry officers sauntering down the Corso, the same coffee-colored jackets of the artillery, the same scarlet trousers of the cavalry; everywhere in that great and many-colored Empire, and at the same moment every evening, as the clocks in the church towers struck nine, the same retreat was sounded, consisting of cheerfully questioning calls and melancholy answers.

Everywhere were to be found the same coffee-houses, with their smoky vaulted ceilings and their dark alcoves where the chess-players sat hunched like strange birds, with their sideboards heavy with colored bottles and shining glasses, presided over by golden-blonde, full-bosomed cashiers. Almost everywhere, in all the coffee-houses of the Empire, there crept with a knee already a little shaky, feet turning outwards, a napkin across his arm, the whiskered waiter, the distant humble image of an old servitor of His Majesty, that mighty whiskered gentleman to whom all Crown Lands, gendarmes, revenue officers, tobacconists, turnpikes, railways, and all his peoples belonged.

And in each Crown Land different songs were sung; peasants wore different clothes; people spoke a different tongue or, in some instances, several different tongues. And what so pleased the Count was the solemn and yet cheerful black-and-yellow that shone with such familiar light amidst so many different colors; the equally solemn and happy *Gott erhalte, God Save the Emperor,* which was native among all the songs of all the peoples, and that particular, nasal, drawling, gentle German of the Austrians, reminding one of the Middle Ages which was always to be picked out again among the varying idioms and dialects of the peoples. Like every Austrian of his day, he loved what was permanent in the midst of constant change, what was familiar amid the unfamiliar. So that things which were alien became native to him without losing their color, and his native land had the eternal magic of the alien.

In his village of Lopatyny the Count was more powerful than any of the administrative branches known to, and feared by, the peasants and the Jews, more powerful than the circuit judge in the nearest small town, more so than the local town mayor himself and more so than any of the senior officers who commanded the troops at the annual maneuvers, requisitioning huts and houses for billets, and generally representing that warlike might which is so much more impressive than actual military power in wartime. It seemed to the people of Lopatyny that "Count" was not only a title of nobility but also quite a high position in local government. In practice they were not far wrong. Thanks to his generally accepted standing, Count Morstin was able to moderate taxes, relieve the sickly sons of Jews from military service, forward requests for favors, relieve punishments meted out to the innocent, reduce punishments which were unduly severe, obtain reductions in railway fares for poor people, secure just retribution for gendarmes, policemen and civil servants who overstepped their position, obtain assistant masterships at the *Gymnasium* for teaching candidates, find jobs as tobacconists, deliverers of registered letters and telegraphists for time-expired NCOs and find "bursaries" for the student sons of poor peasants and Jews.

How happy he was to attend to it all! In order to keep abreast of his duties, he employed two secretaries and three writers. On top of this, true to the tradition of his house, he practiced "seigneurial charity," as it was known in the village. For more than a century the tramps and beggars of the neighborhood had gathered every Friday beneath the balcony of the Morstin manor and received from the footmen copper coins in twists of paper. Usually, the Count would appear on the balcony and greet the poor, and it was as if he were giving thanks to the beggars who thanked him: as if giver and receiver exchanged gifts.

In parenthesis, it was not always goodness of heart which produced all these good works, but one of those unwritten laws common to so many families of the nobility. Their far distant forebears might indeed, centuries before, have practiced charity, help and support of their people out of pure love. Gradually, though, as the blood altered, this goodness of heart had to some extent become frozen and petrified into duty and tradition. Furthermore, Count Morstin's busy willingness to be helpful formed his only activity and distraction. It lent to his somewhat idle life as a *grand seigneur* who, unlike his peers and neighbors, took no interest even in hunting, an object and an aim, a constantly beneficent confirmation of his power. If he had arranged a tobacconist's business for one person, a license for another, a job for a third, an interview for a fourth, he felt at ease not only in his conscience but in his pride. If, however, he proved unsuccessful in his good offices on behalf of one or another of his *protégés,* then his conscience was uneasy and his pride was wounded. And he never gave up; he invariably went to appeal, until his wish—that is, the wish of his *protégés*—had been fulfilled. For this reason the people loved and respected him. For ordinary folk have no real conception of the motives which induce a man of power to help the powerless and the unimportant. People just wish to see a "good master"; and people are often more magnanimous in their childlike trust in a powerful man than is the very man whose magnanimity they credulously assume. It is the deepest and noblest wish of ordinary folk to believe that the powerful must be just and noble.

This sort of consideration was certainly not present in Count Morstin's mind as he dispensed protection, beneficence and justice. But these considerations, which may have led an ancestor here and an ancestor there to the practice of generosity, pity and justice, were still alive and working, in the blood or, as they say today, the "subconscious" of this descendant. And just as he felt himself in duty bound to help those who were weaker than himself, so he exhibited duty, respect and obedience towards those who were higher placed than himself. The person of His Royal and Imperial Majesty was to him for ever a quite uniquely remarkable phenomenon. It would, for example, have been impossible for the Count to consider the Emperor simply as a person. Belief in the hereditary hierarchy was so deep-seated and so strong in Franz

Xaver's soul that he loved the Emperor because of his Imperial, not his human, attributes. He severed all connection with friends, acquaintances or relations if they let fall what he considered a disrespectful word about the Emperor. Perhaps he sensed even then, long before the fall of the monarchy, that frivolous witticisms can be far more deadly than criminal attempts at assassination and the solemn speeches of ambitious and rebellious world reformers; in which case world history would have borne out Count Morstin's suspicions. For the old Austro-Hungarian monarchy died, not through the empty verbiage of its revolutionaries, but through the ironical disbelief of those who should have believed in, and supported, it.

## II

One fine day—it was a couple of years before the Great War, which people now call the World War—Count Morstin was told in confidence that the next Imperial maneuvers were to take place in Lopatyny and the adjacent territory. The Emperor planned to spend a day or two, or a week, or longer in his house. And Morstin flew into a real taking, drove to the town mayor, dealt with the civil police authorities and the urban district council of the neighboring market town, arranged for the policemen and night-watchmen of the entire district to have new uniforms and swords, spoke with the priests of all three confessions, Greek Catholics, Roman Catholics, and the Jewish Rabbi, wrote out a speech for the Ruthenian mayor of the town (which he could not read but had to learn by heart with the help of the schoolteacher), bought white dresses for the little girls of the village and alerted the commanding officers of every regiment in the area. All this so much "in confidence" that in early spring, long before the maneuvers, it was known far and wide in the neighborhood that the Emperor himself would be attending the maneuvers.

At that time Count Morstin was no longer young, but haggard and prematurely gray. He was a bachelor and a misogynist, considered somewhat peculiar by his more robust equals, a trifle "comic" and "from a different planet." Nobody in the district had seen a woman near him, nor had he ever made any attempt to marry. None had seen him drink, gamble or make love. His solitary passion was combating "the problem of nationalities." Indeed it was at this time that the so-called "problem of nationalities" began to arouse the passions. Everybody like himself—whether he wished to, or felt impelled to act as if he wished to—concerned himself with one or other of the many nations which occupied the territory of the old Monarchy. It had been discovered and brought to people's attention in the course of the nineteenth century that in order to possess individuality as a citizen every person must belong to a definite nationality or race. "From humanity, via nationalism to bestiality," the Austrian poet Grillparzer had said. It was just at this time that nationalism was beginning, the stage before the bestiality which we are experiencing today. One could see clearly then that national sentiment sprang from the vulgar turn of mind of all the people who derived from, and corresponded with, the most commonplace attitudes of a modern country. They were generally photographers with a sideline in the volunteer fire brigade, self-styled artists who for lack of talent had found no home in the art academy and in consequence had ended up as sign-painters and paper-hangers, discontented teachers in primary schools who would have liked to teach in secondary schools, apothecaries' assistants who wanted to be doctors, tooth pullers who could not become dentists, junior employees in the Post Office and the railways, bank clerks, woodmen and, generally speaking, anyone with any of the Austrian nationalities who had an unjustifiable claim to a limitless horizon within that bourgeois society. And all these people who had never been anything but Austrians, in Tarnopol, Sarajevo, Brünn, Prague, Czernowitz, Oderburg or Troppau; all these who had never been anything but Austrian, began in accordance with the "Spirit of the Age" to look upon themselves as members of the Polish, Czech, Ukrainian, German, Roumanian, Slovenian and Croatian "nations," and so on and so forth.

At about this time "universal, secret and direct suffrage" was introduced in the Monarchy. Count Morstin detested this as much as he did the concept of "nation."

He used to say to the Jewish publican Solomon Piniowsky, the only person for miles around in whose company he had some sort of confidence, "Listen to me, Solomon! This dreadful Darwin, who says men are descended from apes, seems to be right. It is no longer enough for people to be divided into races, far from it! They want to belong to particular nations. Nationalism; do you hear Solomon?! Even the apes never hit on an idea like that. Darwin's theory still seems to me incomplete. Perhaps the apes are descended from the nationalists since they are certainly a step forward. You know your Bible, Solomon, and you know that it is written there that on the sixth day God created man, not nationalist man. Isn't that so, Solomon?"

"Quite right, *Herr Graf*!" said the Jew, Solomon.

"But," the Count went on, "to change the subject: we are expecting the Emperor this summer. I will give you some money. You will clean up and decorate this place and light up the window. You will dust off the Emperor's picture and put it in the window. I will make you a present of a black and yellow flag with the double eagle on it, and you will fly it from the roof. Is that understood?"

Indeed, the Jew Piniowsky understood, as, moreover, did everybody else with whom the Count had discussed the arrival of the Emperor.

### III

That summer the Imperial maneuvers took place, and His Imperial, Royal and Apostolic Majesty took up residence in Count Morstin's castle. The Emperor was to be seen every morning as he rode out to watch the exercises, and the peasants and Jewish merchants of the neighborhood would gather to see him, this old man who was their ruler. And as soon as he and his suite appeared they would shout *hoch* and *hurra* and *niech zyje,* each in his own tongue. A few days after the Kaiser's departure, the son of a local peasant called upon Count Morstin. This young man, whose ambition was to become a sculptor, had prepared a bust of the Emperor in sandstone. Count Morstin was enchanted. He promised the young sculptor a free place at the Academy of Arts in Vienna.

He had the bust of the Emperor mounted at the entrance to his little castle.

Here it remained, year in, year out, until the outbreak of

the Great War which became known as the World War.

Before he reported for duty as a volunteer, elderly, drawn, bald and hollow-eyed as he had become with the passage of years, Count Morstin had the Emperor's bust taken down, packed in straw and hidden in the cellar.

And there it rested until the end of the war and of the Monarchy, until Count Morstin returned home, until the constitution of the new Polish Republic.

## IV

Count Franz Xaver Morstin had thus come home. But could one call this a homecoming? Certainly, there were the same fields, the same woods, the same cottages and the same sort of peasants—the same *sort,* let it be said advisedly—for many of the ones whom the Count had known had fallen in battle.

It was winter, and one could already feel Christmas approaching. As usual at this time of year, and as it had been in days long before the war, the Lopatinka was frozen, crows crouched motionless on the bare branches of the chestnut trees and the eternal leisurely wind of the Eastern winter blew across the fields onto which the western windows of the house gave.

As the result of the war, there were widows and orphans in the villages: enough material for the returning Count's beneficence to work upon. But instead of greeting his native Lopatyny as a home regained, Count Morstin began to indulge in problematical and unusual meditations on the question of home generally. Now, thought he, since this village belongs to Poland and not to Austria, is it still my home? What, in fact, is home? Is not the distinctive uniform of gendarmes and customs officers, familiar to us since childhood, just as much "home" as the fir and the pine, the pond and the meadow, the cloud and the brook? But if the gendarmes and customs officers are different and fir, pine, brook and pond remain the same, is that still home? Was I not therefore at home in this spot—continued the Count enquiringly—only because it belonged to an overlord to whom there also belonged countless other places of different kinds, all of which I loved? No doubt about it! This unnatural whim of history has also destroyed my private pleasure in what I used to know as home. Nowadays they are talking hereabouts and every-where else of this new fatherland. In their eyes I am a so-called Lackland. I have always been one. Ah! but there was once a fatherland, a real one, for the Lacklands, the only possible fatherland. That was the old Monarchy. Now I am homeless and have lost the true home of the eternal wanderer.

In the false hope that he could forget the situation if he were outside the country, the Count decided to go abroad. But he discovered to his astonishment that he needed a pass-port and a number of so-called visas before he could reach those countries which he had chosen for his journey. He was quite old enough to consider as fantastically childish and dreamlike such things as passports, visas and all the formalities which the brazen laws of traffic between man and man had imposed after the war. However, since Fate had decreed that he was to spend the rest of his days in a desolate dream, and because he hoped to find abroad, in other countries, some part of that old reality in which he had lived before the war, he bowed to the requirements of this ghostly world, took a passport, procured visas and proceeded first to Switzerland, the one country in which he believed he might find the old peace, simply because it had not been involved in the war.

He had known the city of Zurich for many years, but had not seen it for the better part of twelve. He supposed that it would make no particular impact on him, for better or for worse. His impression coincided with the not altogether unjustified opinion of the world, both rather more pampered and rather more adventurous, on the subject of the worthy cities of the worthy Swiss. What, after all, could be expected to happen there? Nevertheless, for a man who had come out of the war and out of the eastern marches of the former Austrian Monarchy, the peace of a city which even before that war had harbored refugees, was almost equivalent to an adventure. Franz Xaver Morstin gave himself up in those first days to the pursuit of long-lost peace. He ate, drank and slept.

One day, however, there occurred a disgusting incident in a Zurich night club, as the result of which Count Morstin was forced to leave the country at once.

At that time there was often common gossip in the newspapers of every country about some wealthy banker who was supposed to have taken in pawn, against a loan to the Austrian royal family, not only the Habsburg Crown Jewels, but also the old Habsburg Crown itself. No doubt about it that these stories came from the tongues and pens of those irresponsible customers known as journalists and even if it were true that a certain portion of the Imperial family's heritage had found its way into the hands of some conscienceless banker, there was still no question of the old Habsburg crown coming into it, or so Franz Xaver Morstin felt that he knew.

So he arrived one night in one of the few bars, known only

to the select, which are open at night in the moral city of
Zurich where, as is well known, prostitution is illegal,
immorality is taboo, the city in which to sin is as boring as it
is costly. Not for a moment that the Count was seeking this
out! Far from it: perfect peace had begun to bore him and to
give him insomnia and he had decided to pass the night-time
away wherever he best could.

He began his drink. He was sitting in one of the few quiet
corners of the establishment. It is true that he was put out by
the newfangled American style of the little red table lamps, by
the hygienic white of the barman's coat which reminded him
of an assistant in an operating theater and by the dyed blonde
hair of the waitress which awoke associations with apothecaries; but to what had he not already accustomed himself,
this poor old Austrian? Even so, he was startled out of the
peace which he had with some trouble arranged for himself
in these surroundings by a harsh voice announcing: "And
here, ladies and gentlemen, is the crown of the Habsburgs!"

Franz Xaver stood up. In the middle of the long bar he
observed a fairly large and animated party. His first glance
informed him that every type of person he hated—although
until then he had no close contact with them—was represented at that table: women with dyed blonde hair in short dresses
which shamelessly revealed ugly knees; slender, willowy young
men of olive complexion, baring as they smiled sets of flawless
teeth such as are to be seen in dental advertisements, disposable
little dancing men, cowardly, elegant, watchful, looking like cun-
ning hairdressers; elderly gentlemen who assiduously but vainly
attempted to disguise their paunches and their bald pates, good-
humored, lecherous, jovial and bow-legged; in short a selection

from that portion of humanity which was for the time being the inheritor of the vanished world, only to yield it a few years later, at a profit, to even more modern and murderous heirs.

One of the elderly gentlemen now rose from the table. First he twirled a crown in his hand, then placed it on his bald head, walked round the table, proceeded to the middle of the bar, danced a little jig, waggled his head and with it the crown, and sang a popular hit of the day, "The sacred crown is worn like this!"

At first Franz Xaver could not make head nor tail of this lamentable exhibition. It seemed to him that the party consisted of decaying old gentlemen with gray hair (made fools of by mannequins in short skirts); chambermaids celebrating their day off; female barflies who would share with the waitresses the profits from the sale of champagne and their own bodies; a lot of good-for-nothing pimps who dealt in women and foreign exchange, wore wide padded shoulders and wide flapping trousers that looked more like women's clothes; and dreadful-looking middlemen who dealt in houses, shops, citizenships, passports, concessions, good marriages, birth certificates, religious beliefs, titles of nobility, adoptions, brothels and smuggled cigarettes. This was the section of society which was relentlessly committed, in every capital city of a Europe which had, as a whole continent, been defeated, to live off its corpse, slandering the past, exploiting the present, promoting the future, sated but insatiable. These were the Lords of Creation after the Great War. Count Morstin had the impression of being his own corpse, and that these people were dancing on his grave. Hundreds and thousands had died in agony to prepare the victory of people like these, and hundreds of thoroughly respectable moralists had prepared the collapse of the old Monarchy, had longed for its fall and for the liberation of the nation-states! And now, pray observe, over the grave of the old world and about the cradles of the newborn nations, there danced the specters of the night from American bars.

Morstin came closer, so as to have a better view. The shadowy nature of these well-covered, living specters aroused his interest. And upon the bald pate of this bowlegged, jigging man he recognized a facsimile—for facsimile it must surely be—of the crown of St. Stephen. The waiter, who was obsequious in drawing the attention of his customers to anything noteworthy, came to Franz Xaver and said, "That is Walakin the banker, a Russian. He claims to own the crowns of all the dethroned monarchies. He brings a different one here every evening. Last night it was the Tsars' crown; tonight it is the crown of St. Stephen."

Count Morstin felt his heart stop beating, just for a second. But during this one second—which seemed to him later to have lasted for at least an hour—he experienced a complete transformation of his own personality. It was as if an unknown, frightening, alien Morstin were growing within him, rising, growing, developing and taking possession not only of his familiar body but, further, of the entire space occupied by the American bar. Never in his life, never since his childhood had Franz Xaver Morstin experienced a fury like this. He had a gentle disposition and the sanctuary which had been vouchsafed him by his position, his comfortable circumstances and the brilliance of his name had until then shielded him from the grossness of the world and from any contact with its meanness. Otherwise, no doubt, he would have learned anger sooner. It was as if he sensed, during that single second that changed him, that the world had changed long before. It was as if he now felt that the change in himself was in fact a necessary consequence of universal change. That much greater than this unknown anger, which now rose up in him, grew and overflowed the bounds of his personality, must have been the growth of meanness in this world, the growth of that baseness which had so long hidden behind the skirts of fawning "loyalty" and slavish servility. It seemed to him, who had always assumed without a second thought that everyone was by nature honorable, that at this instant he had discovered a lifetime of error, the error of any generous heart, that he had given credit, limitless credit. And this sudden recognition filled him with the honest shame which is sister to honest anger. An honest man is doubly shamed at the sight of meanness, first because the very existence of it is shameful, second because he sees at once that he has been deceived in his heart. He sees himself betrayed and his pride rebels against the fact that people have betrayed his heart.

It was no longer possible for him to weigh, to measure, to consider. It seemed to him that hardly any kind of violence could be bestial enough to punish and wreak vengeance on the baseness of the man who danced with a crown on his bald whoremongering head; every night a different crown. A gramophone was blaring out the song from *Hans, who does things with his knee;* the barmaids were shrilling; the young men clapped their hands; the barman, white as a surgeon, rattled among his glasses, spoons and bottles, shook and mixed, brewed and concocted in metal shakers the secret and magical potions of the modern age. He clinked and rattled, from time to time turning a benevolent but calculating eye on the banker's performance. The little red lamps trembled every time the bald man stamped. The light, the gramophone, the noise of the mixer, the cooing and giggling of the women drove Count Morstin into a marvelous rage. The unbelievable happened: for the first time in his life he became laughable and childish. He armed himself with a half-empty bottle of champagne and a blue soda-siphon, then approached the strangers. With his left hand he squirted soda water over the company at the table and with his right hand struck the dancer over the head with the bottle. The banker fell to the ground. The crown fell from his head. And as the Count stooped to pick it up, as it were to rescue the real crown and all that was associated with it, waiters, girls and pimps all rushed at him. Numbed by the powerful scent of the women and the blows of the young men, Count Morstin was finally brought out into the street. There, at the door of the American bar, the obsequious waiter presented the bill, on a silver tray, under the wide heavens and, in a manner of speaking, in the presence of every distant and indifferent star; for it was a crisp winter night.

The next day Count Morstin returned to Lopatyny.

## V

Why—said he to himself during the journey—should I not go back to Lopatyny? Since my world seems to have met with final defeat and I no longer have a proper home it is better that I should seek out the wreckage of my old one!

He thought of the bust of the Emperor Franz Josef which lay in his cellar, and he thought of this, his Emperor's corpse, which had long lain in the Kapuzinergruft.

I was always odd man out, thought he to himself, both in my village and in the neighborhood. I shall remain odd man out.

He sent a telegram to his steward announcing the day of his arrival.

And when he arrived they were waiting for him, as always, as in the old days, as if there had been no war, no dissolution of the Monarchy, no new Polish Republic.

For it is one of the greatest mistakes made by the new—or as they like to call themselves, modern—statesmen that the people (the "nation") share their own passionate interest in world politics. The people in no way lives by world politics, and is thereby agreeably distinguishable from politicians. The people lives by the land, which it works, by the trade which it exercises and by the craft which it understands. (It nevertheless votes at free elections, dies in wars and pays taxes to the Ministry of Finance.) Anyway, this is the way things were in Count Morstin's village of Lopatyny, and the whole of the World War and the complete redrawing of the map of Europe had not altered the opinions of the people of Lopatyny. Why and how? The sound, human sense of the Jewish publicans and the Polish and Ruthenian peasants resented the incomprehensible whims of world history. These whims are abstract: but the likes and dislikes of the people are concrete.

The people of Lopatyny, for instance, had for years known the Counts Morstin, those representatives of the Emperor and the house of Habsburg. New gendarmes appeared, and a tax-levy is a tax-levy, and Count Morstin is Count Morstin. Under the rule of the Habsburgs the people of Lopatyny had been happy or unhappy—each according to the will of God. Independent of all the changes in world history, in spite of republics and monarchies, and what are known as national self-determination or suppression, their life was determined by a good or bad harvest, healthy or rotten fruit, productive or sickly cattle, rich pasture or thin, rain at the right or the wrong season, a sun to bring forth fruit or drought and disaster. The world of the Jewish merchant consisted of good or bad customers; for the publican in feeble or reliable drinkers and for the craftsman it was important whether people did or did not require new roofs, new boots, new trousers, new stoves, new chimneys or new barrels. This was the case, at least in Lopatyny. And in our prejudiced view the whole wide world is not so different from the village of Lopatyny as popular leaders and politicians would like to believe. When they have read the newspapers, listened to speeches, elected officials and talked over the doings of the world with their friends, these worthy peasants, craftsmen and shopkeepers— and in big cities the workmen as well—go back to their houses and their places of work. And at home they find worry or happiness; healthy children or sick children, discontented or peaceable wives, customers who pay well or pay slowly, pressing or patient creditors, a good meal or a bad one, a clean or a dirty bed. It is our firm conviction that ordinary folk do not trouble their heads over world events, however much they may rant and rave about them on Sundays. But this may, of course, be a personal conviction. We have in fact only to report on the village of Lopatyny. These things were as we have described them.

No sooner was Count Morstin home than he repaired at once to Solomon Piniowsky, that Jew in whom innocence and shrewdness went hand in hand, as if they were brother and sister. And the Count asked the Jew, "Solomon, what do you count on in this world?"

"*Herr Graf*," said Piniowsky, "I no longer count on anything at all. The world has perished, there is no Emperor any more, people choose presidents, and that is the same thing as when I pick a clever lawyer for a lawsuit. So the whole people picks a lawyer to defend it. But, I ask myself, *Herr Graf*, before what tribunal? Just a tribunal of other lawyers. And supposing the people have no lawsuit and therefore no need to be defended, we all know just the same that the very existence of these lawyers will land us up to the neck in a lawsuit. And so there will be constant lawsuits. I still have the black and yellow flag, *Herr Graf*, which you gave me as a present. What am I to do with it? It is lying on the floor of my attic. I still have the picture of the old Emperor. What about that, now? I read the newspapers, I attend a bit to business, and a bit to the world. I know the stupid things that are being done. But our peasants have no idea. They simply believe that the old Emperor has introduced new uniforms and set Poland free, that he no longer has his Residence in Vienna, but in Warsaw."

"Let them go on thinking that," said Count Morstin.

And he went home and had the bust of the Emperor Franz Joseph brought up from the cellar. He stood it at the entrance to his house.

And from the following day forward, as though there had been no war and no Polish Republic; as though the old Emperor had not been long laid to rest in the Kapuzinergruft; as though this village still belonged to the territory of the old Monarchy; every peasant who passed by doffed his cap to the sandstone bust of the old Emperor and every Jew who passed by with his bundle murmured the prayer which a pious Jew will say on seeing an Emperor. And this improbable bust—presented in cheap sandstone from the unaided hand of a peasant lad, this bust in the uniform jacket of the dead Emperor, with stars and insignia and the Golden Fleece, all preserved in stone, just as the youthful eye of the lad had seen the Emperor and loved him—won with the passing of time a quite special and particular artistic merit, even in the eyes of Count Morstin. It was as if the passing of time ennobled and improved the work which represented this exalted subject. Wind and weather worked as if with artistic consciousness upon the simple stone. It was as if respect and remembrance also worked upon this portrait, as if every salute from a peasant, every prayer from a believing Jew, had ennobled the unconscious work of the young peasant's hands.

And so the bust stood for years outside Count Morstin's house, the only memorial which had ever existed in the village of Lopatyny and of which all its inhabitants were rightly proud.

The bust meant even more, however, to the Count, who in those days no longer left the village any more. It gave him the impression, whenever he left his house, that nothing had altered. Gradually, for he had aged prematurely, he would stumble upon quite foolish ideas. He would persuade himself for hours at a time, although he had fought through the whole of the greatest of all wars, that this had just been a bad dream, and that all the changes which had followed it were also bad dreams. This in spite of the fact that he saw almost every week how his appeals to officials and judges no longer helped his *protégés* and that these officials indeed made fun of him. He was more infuriated than insulted. It was already well known in the neighboring small town, as in the district, that "old Morstin was half crazy." The story circulated that at home he wore the uniform of a *Rittmeister* of Dragoons, with all his old orders and decorations. One day a neighboring landowner, a certain Count, asked him straight out if this were true.

"Not as yet," replied Morstin, "but you've given me a good idea. I shall put on my uniform and wear it not only at home but out and about."

And so it happened.

From that time on Count Morstin was to be seen in the uniform of an Austrian *Rittmeister* of Dragoons, and the inhabitants of Lopatyny never gave the matter a second thought. Whenever the *Rittmeister* left his house he saluted his Supreme Commander, the bust of the dead Emperor Franz Josef. He would then take his usual route between two little pinewoods along the sandy road which led to the neighboring small town. The peasants who met him would take off their hats and say: "Jesus Christ be praised!" adding *"Herr Graf!"* as if they believed the Count to be some sort of close relative of the Redeemer's, and that two titles were better than one. Alas, for a long time past he had been powerless to help them as he had in the old days. Admittedly the peasants were unable to help themselves. But he, the Count, was no longer a power in the land! And like all those who have been powerful once, he now counted even less than those who had always been powerless: in the eyes of officialdom he almost belonged among the ridiculous. But the people of Lopatyny and its surroundings still believed in him, just as they believed in the Emperor Franz Josef whose bust it was their custom to salute. Count Morstin seemed in no way laughable to the peasants and Jews of

Lopatyny; venerable, rather. They revered his lean, thin figure, his gray hair, his ashen, sunken countenance, and his eyes which seemed to stare into the boundless distance; small wonder, for they were staring into the buried past.

It happened one day that the regional commissioner for Lwow, which used to be called Lemberg, undertook a tour of inspection and for some reason had to stop in Lopatyny. Count Morstin's house was pointed out to him and he at once made for it. To his astonishment he caught sight of the bust of the Emperor Franz Josef in front of the house, in the midst of a little shrubbery. He looked at it for a long while and finally decided to enter the house and ask the Count himself about the significance of this memorial. But he was even more astonished, not to say startled, at the sight of Count Morstin coming towards him in the uniform of a *Rittmeister* of Dragoons. The regional commissioner was himself a "Little Pole"; which means he came from what was formerly Galicia. He had himself served in the Austrian Army. Count Morstin appeared to him like a ghost from a chapter of history long forgotten by the regional commissioner.

He restrained himself and at first asked no questions. As they sat down to table, however, he began cautiously to enquire about the Emperor's memorial.

"Ah, yes," said the Count, as if no new world had been born, "His late Majesty of blessed memory spent eight days in this house. A very gifted peasant lad made the bust. It has always stood here and will do so as long as I live."

The commissioner stifled the decision which he had just taken and said with a smile, as it were quite casually, "You still wear the old uniform?"

"Yes," said Morstin, "I am too old to have a new one made. In civilian clothes, do you know, I don't feel altogether at ease since circumstances became so altered. I'm afraid I might be confused with a lot of other people. Your good health," continued the Count, raising his glass and toasting his guest.

The regional commissioner sat on for a while, and then left the Count and the village of Lopatyny to continue his tour of inspection. When he returned to his Residence he issued orders that the bust should be removed from before Count Morstin's house.

These orders finally reached the mayor (termed *Wojt*) of the village of Lopatyny and therefore, inevitably, were brought to the attention of Count Morstin.

For the first time, therefore, the Count now found himself in open conflict with the new power, of whose existence he had previously hardly taken cognizance. He realized that he was too weak to oppose it. He recalled the scene at night in the American bar in Zurich. Alas, there was no point any more in shutting one's eyes to these new bankers and wearers of crowns, to the new ladies and gentlemen who ruled the world. One must bury the old world, but one must give it a decent burial.

So Count Morstin summoned ten of the oldest inhabitants of the village of Lopatyny to his house—among them the clever and yet innocent Jew, Solomon Piniowsky. There also attended the Greek Catholic priest, the Roman Catholic priest and the Rabbi.

When they were all assembled Count Morstin began the following speech,

"My dear fellow-citizens, you have all known the old

Monarchy, your old fatherland. It has been dead for years, and I have come to realize that there is no point in not seeing that it is dead. Perhaps it will rise again, but old people like us will hardly live to see it. We have received orders to remove, as soon as possible, the bust of the dead Emperor, of blessed memory, Franz Josef the First.

"We have no intention of removing it, my friends!

"If the old days are to be dead we will deal with them as one does deal with the dead: we will bury them.

"Consequently I ask you, my dear friends, to help me bury the dead Emperor, that is to say his bust, with all the ceremony and respect that are due to an Emperor, in three days' time, in the cemetery."

## VI

The Ukranian joiner, Nikita Koldin, made a magnificent sarcophagus of oak. Three dead Emperors could have found accommodation in it.

The Polish blacksmith, Jarowslaw Wojciechowski, forged a mighty double eagle in brass which was firmly nailed to the coffin's lid.

The Jewish Torah scribe, Nuchin Kapturak, inscribed with a goose quill upon a small roll of parchment the blessing which believing Jews must pronounce at the sight of a crowned head, cased it in hammered tin and laid it in the coffin.

Early in the morning—it was a hot summer day, countless invisible larks were trilling away in the heavens and countless invisible crickets were replying from the meadows—the inhabitants of Lopatyny gathered at the memorial to Franz

Josef the First. Count Morstin and the mayor laid the bust to rest in its magnificent great sarcophagus. At this moment the bells of the church on the hill began to toll. All three pastors placed themselves at the head of the procession. Four strong old peasants bore the coffin on their shoulders. Behind them, his drawn saber in his hand, his dragoon helmet draped in field gray, went Count Franz Xaver Morstin, the closest person in the village to the dead Emperor, quite lonely and alone, as becomes a mourner. Behind him, wearing a little round black cap upon his silver hair, came the Jew, Solomon Piniowsky, carrying in his left hand his round velvet hat and raised in his right the black and yellow flag with the double eagle. And behind him the whole village, men and women.

The church bells tolled, the larks trilled and the crickets sang unceasingly.

The grave was prepared. The coffin was lowered with the flag draped over it, and for the last time Franz Xaver Morstin raised his saber in salute to his Emperor.

The crowd began to sob as though the Emperor Franz Josef and with him the old Monarchy and their own old home had only then been buried. The three pastors prayed.

So the old Emperor was laid to rest a second time, in the village of Lopatyny, in what had once been Galicia.

A few weeks later the news of this episode reached the papers. They published a few witticisms about it, under the heading, "Notes from all over."

## VII

Count Morstin, however, left the country. He now lives on the Riviera, an old man and worn out, spending his evenings playing chess and *skat* with ancient Russian generals. He spends an hour or two every day writing his memoirs. They will probably possess no significant literary value, for Count Morstin has no experience as a literary man, and no ambition as a writer. Since, however, he is a man of singular grace and style he delivers himself of a few memorable phrases, such as the following for example, which I reproduce with his permission: "It has been my experience that the clever are capable of stupidity, that the wise can be foolish, that true prophets can lie and that those who love truth can deny it. No human virtue can endure in this world, save only one: true piety. Belief can cause us no disappointment since it promises us nothing in this world. The true believer does not fail us, for he seeks no recompense on earth. If one uses the same yardstick for peoples, it implies that they seek in vain for national virtues, so-called, and that these are even more questionable than human virtues. For this reason I hate nationalism and nation states. My old home, the Monarchy, alone, was a great mansion with many doors and many chambers, for every condition of men. This mansion has been divided, split up, splintered. I have nothing more to seek for, there. I am used to living in a home, not in cabins."

So, proudly and sadly, writes the old Count. Peaceful, self-possessed, he waits on death. Probably he longs for it. For he has laid down in his will that he is to be buried in the village of Lopatyny; not, indeed, in the family vault, but alongside the grave of the Emperor Franz Josef, beside the bust of the Emperor.

# The Legend of the Holy Drinker

TRANSLATED FROM THE GERMAN
BY MICHAEL HOFMANN

# 1

On a spring evening in 1934 a gentleman of mature years descended one of the flights of stone steps that lead from the bridges over the Seine down to its banks. It is there that, as all the world knows and so will hardly need reminding, the homeless poor of Paris sleep, or rather spend the night.

One such poor vagrant chanced to be walking towards the gentleman of mature years, who was incidentally well-dressed and had the appearance of a visitor, disposed to take in the sights of foreign cities. This vagrant looked no less pitiable and bedraggled than any other, but to the elderly well-dressed man he seemed to merit some particular attention: why, we are unable to say.

It was, as already mentioned, evening, and under the bridges on the banks of the river it was rather darker than it was up on the bridges and embankments above. The vagrant was swaying slightly and was clearly the worse for wear. He seemed not to have noticed the elderly, well-dressed gentleman. He, though, had clearly seen the swaying man from some way off, and, far from swaying himself, was striding purposefully towards him. He seemed intent on barring the way of the seedy man. They both came to a halt and confronted one another.

"Where are you going, brother?" asked the elderly, well-dressed gentleman.

The other looked at him for a moment, and said: "I wasn't aware that I had a brother, and I don't know where I'm going."

"Then I will try to show you the way," said the gentleman. "But first will you not be angry with me if I ask you for a rather unusual favor?"

"I am entirely at your service," said the clochard.

"I can see that you are not without blemish. But God has sent you to me. Now, if you'll forgive my saying so, I am sure you could use some money. I have more than enough. Could you tell me how much you require? At least for the immediate future?"

The other reflected for a moment and said: "Twenty francs."

"That can't be enough," replied the gentleman. "I'm sure you require two hundred."

The vagrant took a step back, and for a moment it looked as if he might fall over, but he managed to stay on his feet, if with a little local difficulty. Then he said: "Certainly, I would rather two hundred francs than twenty, but I am a man of honor. You may not have realized as much. I am unable to accept the sum you offer me for the following reasons: firstly, because I don't have the pleasure of knowing you; secondly, because I don't know how and when I would be able to repay you; and thirdly, because there would be no possibility of your asking me to repay you. I have no address. Almost every day finds me under a different bridge. And yet, in spite of that, as

I have assured you, I am a man of honor, albeit of no fixed address."

"I too have no address," replied the elderly gentleman, "and I too may be found under a different bridge every day, and yet I would ask you please to accept the two hundred francs—a bagatelle for a man such as yourself. And as regards its repayment, I should explain why I am unable to refer you, say, to a bank, where you could deposit the money in my account. The fact is that I have recently become a Christian, as a result of reading the story of little St Thérèse de Lisieux. I have a special reverence for her little statue in the Chapelle de Sainte Marie des Batignolles, which you will have no trouble in finding. Therefore, when you next happen to have two hundred francs, and your conscience will not allow you to go on owing me such a paltry sum, I would ask you to go to Sainte Marie des Batignolles, and to leave the money in the hands of the priest who reads the Mass there. For if you owe it to anyone, you owe it to little Thérèse. Don't forget now: Sainte Marie des Batignolles."

"I see," said the clochard, "that you have understood me and my sense of honor perfectly. I give you my word that I will keep my word. But I am only able to go to Mass on a Sunday."

"By all means, on a Sunday," said the elderly gentleman. He took two hundred francs from his wallet, gave them to the swaying fellow, and said: "I thank you!"

"It was a pleasure," replied the other, and immediately vanished into the depths of the gloom.

For it had grown dark in the meantime, down by the river, while up above, on the bridges and quays, the silvery lamps were lighting up, to proclaim the merry Parisian night.

## 2

The well-dressed gentleman also vanished into the darkness. He had indeed experienced the miracle of faith. He had made up his mind to lead a life of poverty. And therefore he lived under bridges.

As for the other fellow, though, he was a drunkard and a toper. His name was Andreas. He lived, like many drunkards, a rather fortuitous existence. It was a long time since he had last had two hundred francs. And perhaps because it was such a long time, he took out a scrap of paper and a stub of pencil, and by the sparse light of one of the few lamps under one of the bridges, he noted down the address of St Thérèse, and the sum of two hundred francs that he now owed her. Then he climbed one of the flights of steps that lead from the Seine's banks to the quays. He knew there was a restaurant there. And he went in, and ate and drank plentifully, and he spent a lot of money, and when he left he took a whole bottle with him for the night, which he intended to spend under the bridge, as usual. Yes, and he picked up a newspaper from a wastepaper bin, not in order to read it, but to wrap himself up in it. For, as all vagrants know, newspapers keep you warm.

## 3

The following morning, Andreas got up rather earlier than usual, for he had slept unusually well. After pondering the matter for a long time, he remembered that he had experienced a miracle yesterday, a miracle. And as it had been a mild night and he seemed to have slept particularly well wrapped up in his newspaper, better than for some time, he decided he would go down to the river and wash, something he hadn't done for many months, in fact not since the onset of the colder weather. Before beginning to undress, though, he felt in the left inside pocket of his jacket, where, if he remembered correctly, there ought still to be some tangible evidence of the miracle. Then he set about looking for a secluded spot on the banks of the Seine, so that he might at least wash his face and neck. However, embarrassed at finding himself in plain view of people, of poor people such as himself (derelicts, as he now suddenly thought of them), he quickly abandoned his original plan, and made do with merely dipping his hands into the water. Then he put his jacket on again, felt once more for the bank-note in his left inside pocket, and, feeling thoroughly cleansed, yes, positively transformed, he set forth.

He set forth into the day, into one of his typical days, such as he had now been passing since the beginning of time, resolved once more to direct his steps to the familiar Rue des Quatre Vents, to the Russian-Armenian restaurant Tari-Bari, where he was in the habit of investing in cheap liquor whatever little money had come his way.

But, at the first newspaper kiosk he passed, he stopped, attracted initially by the illustrations on the covers of some of the weekly magazines, but then also suddenly gripped by curiosity to learn what day it was today, what date and what day of the week. So he bought himself a newspaper, and saw that it was a Thursday, and he suddenly remembered that the day on which he was born was also a Thursday, and, regardless of the date, he decided to make this particular Thursday his birthday. And, already full of a childish feeling of excitement and celebration, he decided unhesitatingly to follow some good, yes, some noble prompting, and for once not go to the Tari-Bari, but instead, newspaper in hand, to seek out some classier establishment, where he would order a roll and some coffee—perhaps inspirited with a jigger of rum.

So, proudly, in spite of his tattered clothing, he walked into a respectable bistro and sat down at a table—he, who for so long had only stood at bars, or rather propped his elbow on them. He sat. And since his chair was facing a mirror, he could hardly avoid looking at his reflection in it, and it was as though he were making his own acquaintance again after a long absence. He was shocked. Immediately he realized why for the last few years he had been so distrustful of mirrors. It was not good to see evidence of his own dissipation with his own eyes. For as long as he had been able to avoid seeing it, it was either as though he had no face at all, or still had the old one from the time before he had become dissipated.

Now, though, he was shocked, especially when he compared his own physiognomy with those of the sleek and respectable men who were seated round him. It was fully a week since he had last had a shave—a rough and ready one, as was usually the case, administered to him by one of his fellows, who would occasionally agree to shave a brother-vagrant for a few coppers. Now, though, in view of his decision to begin a new life, nothing less than a real shave would do. He decided to go to a proper barber's shop before going on with his breakfast.

He suited the action to the thought, and went to a barber.

When he returned to the tavern, he found his former place occupied, and he was now only able to get a distant view of himself in the mirror. But it was enough for him to see that he had been smartened up, rejuvenated, become a new man. Yes, his face seemed to be giving off a sort of radiance which made the tattiness of his clothes seem irrelevant— the ripped shirt-front, and the red-and-white striped foulard he wound over his frayed collar.

So he sat down again, our Andreas, and in the spirit of his renewal he ordered his "café, arrosé rhum," in the confident tone of voice that had long ago once been his, and which now returned to him, like an old sweetheart. The waiter served him, he thought, with a show of esteem that was only accorded to respectable guests. This particularly gratified our Andreas—it boosted his self-esteem, and strengthened him in the conviction that today was indeed his birthday.

A gentleman, who had been sitting alone at a table close to that of our clochard, had been studying him for a while, and now turned to him and addressed him as follows: "Would you be interested in earning some money? You could do some work for me. You see, we're moving house tomorrow. You could help my wife and the removal men. You look as though you have the strength for it. Are you free tomorrow? Would you like to?"

"Yes, by all means," replied Andreas.

"And how much would you expect to be paid for two days' work? Tomorrow and Saturday. Because, you see, I've got rather a large flat, and the one we're moving into is even bigger. There's stacks of furniture too. I won't be able myself to help, as I'll be busy looking after the shop."

"I'm just the man for the job!" said the vagrant.

"Would you care for a drink?" asked the gentleman.

And he ordered two Pernods, they clinked glasses, the gentleman and Andreas, and they also fixed the rate for the job: it was to be two hundred francs.

"Shall we have another?" asked the gentleman, after finishing his Pernod.

"Yes, but let me buy this one," said the vagrant Andreas. "You don't know me, but I'm a man of principle. An honest worker. Take a look at my hands!"—and he held out his hands for inspection—"They may be dirty and calloused, but they're real working-man's hands."

"That's what I like to see!" said the gentleman. He had twinkling eyes, a pink plump baby face and, smack in the middle of it, a little black moustache. All in all, he was a friendly chap, and Andreas took a liking to him.

So they drank together, and Andreas paid for the second round. And when the baby-faced man got up, Andreas saw that he was extremely fat. He took a visiting-card from his wallet, and wrote his address on it. And then he took a hundred-franc note from the same wallet, and handed both together to Andreas, saying: "To be sure you'll turn up tomorrow! Tomorrow morning at eight, all right? Don't forget! I'll pay you the rest when you're finished! And then we'll have another apéritif together! All right? Cheerio, friend!" And with that he was gone, the fat gentleman with the baby face, and nothing surprised Andreas more than the fact that he had produced his address from the same pocket as his money. Well, seeing as *he* now had some money, and the prospect of more to come, he decided to buy a wallet himself. With this in mind, he set off in search of a leather-goods shop. In the first such shop he came across, he saw a young sales-girl. He thought she looked very attractive, the way she stood behind the counter, wearing a black dress with a white apron tied across her bosom, the mop of curls on her head and the heavy gold bracelet on her right wrist. He took his hat off to her, and said breezily: "I'm looking for a wallet." The girl cast a cursory glance at his tattered clothing, not in any spirit of disapproval, simply to assess the customer in front of her. Because in her shop, she sold wallets that were expensive, moderately expensive and very cheap. Without any more ado, she climbed up a ladder and took down a box from the topmost shelf. That was where those wallets were kept that customers sometimes brought in, in part-exchange for new ones. Andreas happened to notice that the girl had very shapely legs, and that her feet were in very trim little shoes, and he remembered those half-forgotten times when he himself had stroked such calves and kissed such feet. The faces he had forgotten, he had no recollection of the faces of the women— with one single exception, namely the one for whose sake he had gone to prison. In the meantime, the girl climbed down from the ladder, and opened the box, and he picked one of the wallets that were lying at the very top, barely looking at it. He paid, put his hat back on, and smiled at the girl and the girl smiled back at him. Rather absent-mindedly, he put the new wallet in his pocket, beside his money. It suddenly seemed to have no point, this wallet. On the other hand, the ladder, and the legs and feet of the girl filled his mind. Therefore he directed his steps towards Montmartre, in search of those places where he had once found pleasure. In a narrow and steep little lane, he found the bar where the girls were. He sat down at a table with several of them, bought a round of drinks, and chose one of the girls, in fact the one who was sitting next to him. They went up to her room. And even though it was only afternoon, he slept until the following morning—and, because the *patronne* was feeling generous, she let him sleep on.

That morning, the Friday, he went to work for the fat gentleman. His job was to help the lady of the house to pack, and, even though the furniture removal men were doing their work, there was more than enough, both arduous and less arduous, to keep Andreas busy. In the course of the day, he felt the strength returning to his muscles, and he took pleasure in his work. He had grown up working, he had been a coalminer like his father, and briefly a farmer like his father before him. If only the lady of the house hadn't got on his nerves so much, giving him pointless instructions, telling him to be in two places at once, so that he didn't know whether he was coming or going. But he could appreciate that she was agitated too. It couldn't have been easy for her, moving house just like that, and maybe she wasn't sure about the new place either. She stood there dressed to go out, in coat and hat and gloves, with her handbag and umbrella, even though she must have known that she would be remaining in the old house all that day and night, and even some of the next day as well. From time to time she would paint her lips, and that too Andreas could well understand. Naturally—she was a lady.

Andreas worked all day. When he had finished, the lady of the house said to him: "Come punctually at seven o'clock tomorrow." She took a little purse full of coins from her handbag. Her fingers scrabbled about in it for a long time, picking up a ten-franc piece then dropping it again, before settling instead on a five-franc piece. "Here's a little something for you!" she said. "But," she added, "you're not to spend it all on drink, and be sure to be here in good time tomorrow!"

Andreas thanked her, left and spent the money—but no more—on drink. He spent the night in a small hotel.

He was woken up at six in the morning. And he went to work feeling fresh and alert.

4

He arrived even before the removal men. The lady of the house was already standing there, exactly as on the previous day, in hat and gloves, as though she hadn't gone to bed at all, and she said to him pleasantly: "I can see you took my advice, and didn't spend the whole of your tip on drink."

Andreas got to work. Later he went with the lady to the new house they were moving into, and waited till the friendly man came home, and paid him the second installment of his wage.

"Now for that drink I promised you," said the gentleman. "Let's go."

But the lady of the house wouldn't allow it, she stood between them and said to her husband: "Dinner's ready." And so Andreas went away alone, and that evening he ate and drank alone, and afterwards he visited another couple of bars. He drank a lot, but he didn't get drunk, and he was careful not to spend too much money, because the next day, mindful of his promise, he wanted to go to the Chapelle de Sainte Marie des Batignolles, and pay at least some of his debt to little Thérèse. But he did drink just enough to cloud his judgment, and make him lose his pauper's infallible instinct for the very cheapest hotel in the *quartier.*

So he went into a slightly more expensive hotel, where, because he had no luggage, and his clothes were in a poor state, he was made to pay in advance. But he wasn't bothered by that, and he slept peacefully until the following morning. He was woken up by the sound of bells tolling in a nearby church, and straightaway it came to him what an important day it was today: it was Sunday, and he had to go to little Thérèse and pay his debt. He quickly pulled his clothes on, and hurried over to the square where the church was. Even so, he reached it too late, because when he arrived the congregation was just emerging from the church after the ten o'clock service. He asked when the next Mass would begin, and was told at noon. He felt at a bit of a loose end, standing around outside the church. There was a whole hour to wait, and he would have preferred not to spend it on the street. So he looked around for some place where he might wait in greater comfort, and saw a bistro diagonally across the square from the church, and decided to spend the hour till Mass there instead.

With the assurance of a man who knows he has money in his pocket, he ordered a Pernod, and with the assurance of a man who has drunk a good many of them in the course of his life, he drank it. He drank another, and a third, adding less water each time. By the time the fourth was served to him, he had no idea whether he had had two glasses, or five or even six. Nor could he remember what he was doing in this café or in this part of town. All he knew was that there was some obligation he had to discharge, some honorable obligation, and he paid, got up, and had walked steadily out of the door when he caught sight of the church facing him across the square, and remembered in a flash where he was and why and to accomplish what.

He was just about to take a step towards the church when he suddenly heard the sound of his name. A voice was calling "Andreas," a woman's voice. It reached him from another age. He stopped and turned his head to the right, where the voice was coming from. And straightaway he recognized the face for whose sake he had gone to prison. It was Caroline.

Caroline! She was wearing clothes and a hat he had never seen her in before, but it was still the same face, and he threw himself into her arms, which she had quickly opened wide to receive him. "What a coincidence," she said. And it was really her voice, the voice of Caroline.

"Are you on your own?" she asked.

"Yes," he said, "I'm alone."

"Come on then, we need to have a talk," she said.

"But, but," he replied, "I've got a rendezvous."

"With a woman?" she asked.

"Yes," he said timidly.

"Who with?"

"With little Thérèse," he replied.

"Never mind her," said Caroline.

Just at that moment a taxi drove by, and Caroline stopped it by waving her umbrella at it. She gave the cabbie an address, and before Andreas quite realized what was happening, he was sitting in the cab with Caroline, driving away, racing away, as it seemed to Andreas, going through a mixture of familiar and unfamiliar streets, to God knows where!

They left the city altogether, and stopped in a landscape, or rather in front of a cultivated garden that was pale green, the green of spring to come. There was a discreet restaurant tucked away behind some almost leafless trees.

Caroline got out first; with her familiar rapacious steps, she got out first, clambering over his knees. She paid, and he followed her. They went into the restaurant and sat side by side on a bench upholstered in green velvet, as in younger days, before he'd gone to prison. She ordered for them both, as she always did; she looked at him and he was afraid to look at her.

"Where have you been all this time?" she asked.

"All over the place," he said. "Nowhere really. I've only been back at work again for two days. All the time we didn't see each other I was drinking and sleeping under bridges like a clochard. I expect you've had a better life. With men," he added, after a pause.

"You can talk," she retorted. "Drunk and out of work and sleeping under bridges you may be, but somehow you still find the time and the opportunity to meet this Thérèse of yours. If I hadn't happened to come along, I expect you'd have gone off with her."

He made no reply, and in fact said nothing at all until they had both finished their meat course, and the cheese had arrived, and the fruit. Just as he was emptying his glass of wine, he was again gripped by the sudden feeling of panic that he had so often felt when he was living with Caroline, years ago. Again, he felt like running away from her, and he called out: "Waiter, the bill please!" But she quickly cut in: "No, waiter, that's my affair!" The waiter, a wise man who had been around, said: "I heard the gentleman call first." And so it was Andreas who paid. He took all the money from his left inside jacket pocket, and after paying, he saw with horror— somewhat diminished by the wine he had drunk—that he no longer had the full sum he owed the little saint. But then again, he comforted himself, so many miracles are happening to me these days, just one after another, that surely I'll be able to get the money together and pay her back next week.

"So, I see you're a rich man," said Caroline when they were outside. "I suppose you've got that little Thérèse working for you?"

Again, he made no reply, and so she was convinced that her suspicion was well-founded. She demanded to be taken to the cinema. He took her to the cinema. It was the first film he'd seen in ages. In fact it was so long since he'd seen one that he could barely follow it, and he fell asleep on Caroline's shoulder. Then they went on to a dance-hall where there was an accordionist, and it was so long since he'd last danced that he didn't know how to dance properly any more when he took to the floor with Caroline. Other dancers kept cutting in and taking her away from him, for she was still young and desirable. He sat by himself at a table and drank Pernod, and it felt just like old times, when Caroline would go off dancing with other men, and he would sit and drink by himself. Finally he had enough, and he got up, pulled her violently away from her partner, and said: "We're going home now!" He gripped her neck, refused to let go, and paid and went home with her. She lived nearby.

It was all just like old times again, just like the old times before he'd gone to prison.

## 5

He woke up very early in the morning. Caroline was still asleep. A solitary bird twittered outside the open window. He lay there for a while with open eyes, no more than a couple of minutes.

During those minutes he was thinking. It seemed to him that not for a long time had so many remarkable things happened to him as now, in the space of this single week. He turned his head abruptly and saw Caroline lying beside him. He saw what he had failed to notice yesterday, at their meeting: that she had aged; pale and puffy and breathing heavily, she slept on into the morning like a woman past her best. He recognized the changes wrought by the years, which seemed to have passed him by. But he also felt the changes in his heart, and he decided to get up immediately, without waking Caroline, and to leave just as fortuitously, or rather just as fatefully, as the two of them had run into one another yesterday. He quietly dressed and went off, into another day, another of his familiar days.

Or rather, into an unfamiliar sort of day. Because when he felt in his left inside jacket pocket, where he used to keep whatever money he had managed to find or to earn, he noticed that all he had left was a fifty-franc note and some loose change. And at that, he, who for many years had not known the meaning of money, and had not been remotely interested in what it might mean—at that, he was taken aback, in the way that a man would be taken aback who expected to have money in his pocket at all times, and who suddenly found himself in the unwonted position of having very little. Suddenly, on the gray, empty pavement of early morning, he, who had had no money whatsoever for months, he seemed to himself to have become poor because he didn't have quite as many notes in his pocket as he had had in the last couple of days. It seemed to him that the time of his impecuniousness was terribly remote, and that what he had done was to take the sum which should have been there to guarantee an appropriate standard of living for himself, and spend it recklessly and rather frivolously on Caroline.

It made him angry with Caroline. And all at once he, to whom the possession of money had never meant a thing, began to have a sense of what money was worth. All at once, he felt that the possession of a single fifty-franc note was demeaning to a man such as himself, and that, to appreciate his true worth again, he urgently needed to be able to reflect on the subject at leisure, and over a glass of Pernod.

He identified the most welcoming of the circumjacent hostelries, sat down and ordered a Pernod. Over his drink, he recalled that he was actually living in Paris without a residence permit, and he checked through his papers. And there he found that he had in fact been expelled from the country, because he had come to France as a coalminer, from Olschowice in Polish Silesia.

## 6

Then, laying his tattered papers out on the table in front of him, he remembered that he had come here one day, many years ago, because he had read an announcement in the news-paper saying that they were looking for coalminers in France. All his life he had longed to go to far-off places. And so he had gone to work in the mines at Quebecque, and he had sub-let a room from some compatriots of his, a married cou-ple by the name of Shebiec. And he had fallen in love with the wife, and one day the husband had tried to kill her, and so he, Andreas, had killed the husband. Thereupon he had gone to prison for two years. The wife was Caroline.

All this was going through Andreas's head as he looked at his now invalid documents. And then he felt such unhappiness that he ordered another Pernod.

When he finally got up, he felt hungry, but it was hunger of a particular sort that only affects drunkards. It is a rather specialized type of craving (not for food at all) that only lasts for a few moments, and that can be immediately stilled if the person who suffers it imagines to himself the exact drink he feels like at that exact moment.

Andreas had long since forgotten his surname. But now, after he had been looking at his invalid papers, he remembered it. It was Kartak. His full name was Andreas Kartak. And he felt as though he had rediscovered himself after many years.

But he still felt a little angry with fate for making it impossible for him to earn any more money, by refusing to direct the fat, baby-faced man with the moustache to this cafe, when it had sent him to that other one. There is really nothing that people get used to so readily as miracles, once they have experienced them two or three times. Yes! In fact, such is human nature that people begin to feel betrayed when they don't keep getting all those things that a chance and fleeting circumstance once bestowed on them. People are like that— so why should Andreas be any different? He spent the rest of the day in various other establishments, and was soon quite reconciled to the fact that the age of miracles he had lately experienced was now, finally, at an end, and that the preceding age had resumed. And so, with his heart set on that slow decline for which a drunkard is always available—and which no sober person can possibly understand!—Andreas took himself back to the banks and bridges of the Seine.

There he slept, half in the daytime, half at night, as he had been used to doing for over a year, every so often managing to borrow a bottle of brandy from one or other of his *confrères*—until the Thursday night.

During the night he dreamed that St Thérèse came to him as a little girl with fair curls, and said to him: "Why didn't you come and see me on Sunday?" And the little saint looked just the way he had imagined his own daughter would look, many years ago. And he had no daughter! And in his dream, he said to little Thérèse: "That's no way to talk to me! Have you forgotten that I'm your father?" The girl answered: "Sorry, father, but will you please, please come and see me on Sunday, the day after tomorrow, at Sainte Marie des Batignolles."

On the morning after his dream, he rose refreshed, as he had done a week earlier, when the miracles were still happening to him, as though this dream was itself a miracle. He felt once more like going to the river and washing himself. But before taking off his jacket to that end, he looked in the left inside pocket, in the vague hope that there might still be some money there that he had perhaps overlooked. He reached into his jacket pocket, and while he didn't find any banknotes, there was still the leather wallet that he had bought some days earlier. He took it out. It really was extremely cheap and tatty—but what else could be expected from a second-hand one? Split leather. Cow's leather. He looked at it, because he could no longer remember having bought it, or when or where. How did I come by that? he asked himself. Finally he opened it, and saw that it had two compartments. Curious, he peered into both of them, and saw that one contained a banknote. He took it out. It was one thousand francs.

He put the thousand francs in his trouser pocket, and went down to the bank of the Seine, where, indifferent to being watched by any of his fellow-unfortunates, he washed his face, yes, and his neck too, almost joyfully. Then he put on his jacket again, and went out into the day, a day which he began by going into a *tabac* to buy cigarettes.

Now, he had enough change still left to pay for the cigarettes, but he didn't know when he would get a chance to change the one-thousand-franc bill that had so miraculously turned up in his wallet. Because he was still able to appreciate that in the eyes of the world, or in the eyes of those that have authority in the world, there was a considerable inconsistency between his clothes and his overall appearance, and the possession of a one-thousand-franc banknote. Nevertheless, heartened by this renewed miracle, he decided he would show the banknote. At the same time, drawing on the remains of his prudence, he would say to the man at the cash-till in the *tabac*: "If you can't change a thousand francs, I've got it in change too. But I would be glad to have it changed."

To Andreas's astonishment the patron of the *tabac* said: "No, on the contrary! I need a one-thousand-franc note, and your coming is most opportune." And the man changed the one thousand francs. Then Andreas stayed awhile at the bar of the *tabac,* and drank three glasses of white wine; an expression of his gratitude to fate for the miracle.

## 7

While he was standing at the bar, he noticed a framed drawing on the wall, behind the broad back of his host, and the drawing reminded him of an old school friend at

Olschowice. He asked the patron: "Who is that? I have a feeling I know him." Thereupon the patron and the other customers standing at the bar all burst out laughing. "What!" they shouted to one another. "He doesn't know who that is!"

Because, of course, as any normal person would have known, it was Kanjak, the great footballer from Silesia. But then how could a man who slept under bridges, an alcoholic like our Andreas, have known that? Feeling ashamed of himself anyway, particularly because he had just had his one-thousand-franc note changed, Andreas muttered: "Of course I know him, he even happens to be a friend of mine. It's just not a terribly good likeness." And, to avoid any further questions, he quickly paid and left.

Now, though, he was genuinely hungry. He made for the nearest restaurant, ate and drank red wine with his meal, had cheese and then coffee, and thought he would spend the afternoon at the cinema. Only he wasn't quite sure which one to go to. But knowing that he had as much money on him at that moment as any of the prosperous types passing him on the pavement, he headed for the great boulevards. Between the Opera and the Boulevard des Capucines he looked for a film he might enjoy, and finally he found one. The poster advertising the film showed a man obviously bent on meeting his death in some far-distant adventure. It described him crawling through the desert under the searing rays of an implacable sun. That was the film for Andreas. He sat in the cinema, watching the man crossing the scorching desert. Andreas was just on the point of finding the hero an admirable character, and identifying with him, when the film abruptly took a happy turn, and the man in the desert was rescued by a passing caravan of scientific researchers, and whisked back to the cradle of European civilization. Whereupon Andreas lost all respect for the hero. He was about to get up and leave when there appeared on the screen the image of the school friend whose picture he had seen a little earlier, behind the proprietor's back, when he had been propping up the bar. It was Kanjak the great footballer. Seeing him on the screen reminded Andreas that once, twenty years ago, he and Kanjak had shared a school bench, and he decided to make inquiries the next morning as to whether his old friend was presently in Paris.

For our Andreas had no less than nine hundred and eighty francs in his pocket.

And that is a not inconsiderable sum.

## 8

However, before he had even left the cinema, it occurred to him that there was actually no compelling reason why he should wait till tomorrow morning to find out the address of his friend and classmate; particularly in view of the rather large sum he had in his pocket.

Having so much money left had given Andreas such confidence that he decided to begin his inquiries for the address of his friend, the celebrated footballer Kanjak, right away, at the cashier's desk. He imagined he might perhaps have to go to the cinema manager to get an answer. But no! There was no one in all Paris so well known as the footballer Kanjak! Even the doorman knew where he lived. He lived in a hotel on the Champs-Élysées. The doorman gave him its name; and our Andreas immediately set off there.

It was a small, quiet, distinguished hotel, just the sort of hotel where footballers and boxers, the elite of our time, like to live. Andreas felt rather odd as he stood in the foyer, and in the eyes of the hotel staff, he looked rather odd too. Still, they told him that the celebrated footballer Kanjak was at home, and was prepared to come down to the foyer straightaway.

And come down he did, a couple of minutes later, and the two of them recognized each other right away. They began exchanging old memories of their schooldays even as they stood there, and then they went out to eat together, and there was great merriment between them. They went out to eat together, and it so happened that the celebrated footballer asked his dissolute friend: "Why are you looking so dissolute, and what are those rags you're wearing?"

"It would be a terrible thing," replied Andreas, "if I were to tell you how that came to pass. And it would greatly impair our mutual joy at this happy reunion of ours. So don't let's talk about that. Let's talk about more cheerful matters instead."

"I've got an awful lot of suits," said the celebrated footballer Kanjak, "and I would be only too glad to let you have one of them. We shared a bench at school, and you let me copy your answers. What's a suit, compared to that! Where shall I have it sent?"

"You can't," replied Andreas, "because I haven't got an address. For some time now, I've been living under the bridges on the banks of the Seine."

"Very well," said the footballer Kanjak, "in that case we'll rent a room for you, expressly so that I can give you a suit. Come along!"

When they had eaten, they went along, and the footballer Kanjak rented a room, and the price of it was twenty-five francs per day, and it was situated near the marvelous church in Paris that goes by the name of "Madeleine."

## 9

The room was on the fifth floor, and Andreas and the footballer had to take the lift up. Of course, Andreas had no luggage, but neither the porter nor the lift-boy nor anyone else on the hotel staff expressed any surprise at that. The whole thing was simply a miracle, and the nuts and bolts of a miracle have nothing miraculous about them. When they were both up in the room, the footballer Kanjak said to his former neighbor in class Andreas: "I expect you need some soap."

"Oh," replied Andreas, "I can get by without soap. I plan to stay here for a week without soap, but I'll still wash. But what I would like is for us to order something to drink, in honor of the room."

And the footballer called for a bottle of cognac, which they emptied between them. Then they left the room, and took a taxi up to Montmartre, to the café where the girls sat, and which Andreas had only lately visited by himself. After sitting there for a couple of hours, exchanging memories of their schooldays, the footballer took Andreas home, that is, to the hotel room he had rented for him, and he said: "It's late now. I'll leave you to yourself. Tomorrow I'll send you two suits. And—do you need money?"

"No," said Andreas, "I've got nine hundred and eighty francs, and that's a sizeable sum. You go home!"

"I'll drop round in a day or two," said the footballer, his friend.


## 10

The room in which Andreas now found himself staying was number eighty-nine. As soon as he was alone, he sat down in the comfortable armchair, which was covered in pink rep, and began to take stock of his surroundings. First he looked at the red silk wall-covering, with its pattern of pale gold parrots' heads, then the door with three ivory doorknobs on its right hand side, the bedside table and the reading lamp on it with its dark green shade, and a second door which had a white door knob, that seemed to have something mysterious behind it, or mysterious at any rate to Andreas. In addition there was a black telephone by the bed, so handily placed that one could lie on the bed and reach across to pick up the receiver quite comfortably. After studying the room for a long time, intent on acquainting himself with it, Andreas suddenly felt a keen curiosity. The second door with the white door knob irritated him, and in spite of his timidity and the fact that he was unaccustomed to the ways of hotel rooms, he got up, determined to see what it might open on to. He had naturally assumed it would be locked. How surprised he was to find that it opened easily, almost invitingly!

He saw before him a bathroom with gleaming tiles, and a tub white and shimmering, and a toilet, and, in short, what might have been termed in his circles a convenience.

At that moment he felt a pressing need to wash, and he turned on both the taps and filled the tub with hot and cold water. As he undressed to get into it, he regretted that he didn't have a change of shirt, because when he took off his shirt he saw that it was exceedingly dirty, and he already dreaded the moment when he would have to get out of the bath and back into his shirt.

He climbed into the bath, conscious of what a long time it was since he had last washed. He bathed gleefully, got out, got into his clothes, and then didn't know what to do with himself. More out of perplexity than curiosity, he opened the door of his room, went out into the corridor, and saw a woman on the point of leaving her room, as he had just done. She was young and beautiful. Indeed, she reminded him of the sales girl in the shop where he had bought his wallet, and also slightly of Caroline, and so he said hello to her and bowed, and when she nodded back to him, he felt emboldened and said to her straight out: "I think you're beautiful."

"I like you as well," she replied, "but now you must excuse me! Perhaps we'll see each other tomorrow." And she disappeared down the dark corridor. He, though, suddenly in need of love, looked to see what the number was on her door.

It was number eighty-seven. He made a note of it in his heart.

## 11

He returned to his room and waited and listened. He felt absolutely determined not to wait till the morning to see the beautiful girl again. The almost uninterrupted stream of mir-

acles of the last few days had convinced him that he must be
in a state of grace; but by that same token, he believed himself entitled to a little excess of zeal on his own behalf, and he
rather thought he would pre-empt grace, out of deference to
it, as it were, and without causing it the slightest offense. So
when he thought he could hear the quiet footfall of the girl
from room eighty-seven in the corridor, he carefully opened
the door of his room by a handbreadth, and saw that it really
was her, going back into her room. What he had failed to realize, though, as a consequence of long years of desuetude, was
the by no means unimportant circumstance that the beautiful girl had observed his little act of espionage. Consequently,
as profession and experience had taught her to do, she quickly
produced a semblance of order in her room, switched off the
main overhead light, lay down on the bed and picked up a
book and began reading it; unfortunately it was a book she
had already read long ago.

A few moments later, as expected, she heard a quiet knock
on her door, and Andreas stepped into her room. He remained
standing by the door, merely awaiting the invitation to step a
little closer which he was sure would not be long in coming.
However, the pretty girl didn't move; she didn't even put her
book aside, she only asked: "And what brings you here?"

Andreas, his confidence boosted by bath, soap, armchair,
wall-covering, parrot's heads and suit, replied: "I couldn't wait
till tomorrow to see you again, my dear."

The girl made no reply.

Andreas moved a little nearer, asked what she was reading
and observed with frankness: "Books don't interest me."

"I'm passing through," said the girl on the bed, "I'm only

staying till Sunday. On Monday I have to appear in Cannes."

"As what?" asked Andreas.

"I dance in a night-club. I'm Gabby. Haven't you ever heard of me?"

"Of course, I've seen your name in the newspapers," lied Andreas—and he was even going to add: the newspapers I sleep in. But he didn't.

He sat down on the edge of the bed, and the pretty girl didn't object. She eventually put away her book, and Andreas stayed in room eighty-seven till morning.

## 12

On the Saturday morning, he awoke with the firm resolve not to leave the beautiful girl until it was time for her to go. Yes, and the fragrant thought bloomed in his mind that he might even travel down to Cannes with her, because, like all poor people (and more especially, like all poor people who also drink), he was inclined to take the small sums of money in his pocket for large ones. So, in the morning, he counted up his nine hundred and eighty francs. And since they were in a wallet, and the wallet was in a new suit, the sum seemed to him to be ten times what it actually was. As a result, he wasn't at all put out, when, an hour after he'd left her, the pretty girl walked straight into his room without knocking, and, when she asked him how they would spend their Saturday together, he said, at a venture, "Fontainebleau." It was like a name he had heard in a dream. He had no idea how and why it came to trip off his tongue now.

So they took a taxi and drove out to Fontainebleau, and it

turned out that the beautiful girl knew of a good restaurant, where they served good food and fine wines. And the waiter there knew her, and she was on first name terms with him. And if our Andreas had been of a jealous disposition, it might have made him angry. But he wasn't jealous, and so he didn't get angry. They spent some time eating and drinking, and then they drove back to Paris, again in a taxi, and suddenly they saw the glittering expanse of the evening in Paris ahead of them, and they didn't know what to do with it, and they were just two people who didn't belong together, whom fate had simply thrown together. The night stretched out ahead of them like an empty desert.

And they were at a loss what to do together, having rather frivolously squandered the principal experience that a man and woman may have together. And so they decided to avail  themselves of the facility reserved to people in our own century when they don't know what to do—they went to the cinema. And they sat there, and it wasn't pitch-black, it wasn't even dark, in fact it could barely be called half-dark. And they held hands, the girl and our friend Andreas. But his hand felt noncommittal, and it embarrassed him. His own hand. When the interval came, he decided to take the beautiful girl out into the foyer for a drink, and they went out and they drank. And he had no interest whatever in the film any more. They went back to their hotel feeling awkward and constrained.

The following morning, the Sunday, Andreas woke up fully aware of his obligation to repay the money. He got up rather more quickly than he had done on the previous morning, with such alacrity in fact that the beautiful girl was startled out of her sleep, and asked, "Why the hurry, Andreas?"

"I have a debt to repay," said Andreas.

"What? Today? On a Sunday?" asked the beautiful girl.

"Yes, today, Sunday," replied Andreas.

"Is it a man or a woman you owe money to?"

"A woman," said Andreas, a little hesitantly.

"What's her name?"

"Thérèse."

Thereupon the beautiful girl leapt out of bed, clenched both her fists and started pummeling Andreas with them.

He fled the room, left the hotel, and, without any further deviation, made straight for Sainte Marie des Batignolles, completely confident that today at last he would be able to repay little Thérèse her two hundred francs.

### 13

Now, as providence would have it—or, as less devout people would say, luck—Andreas once more arrived just too late for the ten o'clock Mass. And, not unnaturally, he once again caught sight of the bistro across the square, where he had gone to drink on the previous occasion, and it was there that he went this time as well.

He ordered a drink. But, canny man that he was, as all the poor people in the world are canny, even after they have been showered with one miracle after another, he first checked the state of his wallet, and took it out of his breast pocket. And he saw that his nine hundred and eighty francs were almost completely gone.

He had only two hundred and fifty left. He thought awhile, and realized that the beautiful girl in the hotel must have taken his money. But our Andreas wasn't at all upset by that. He told himself that enjoyment had to be paid for, that he had enjoyed himself, and that he therefore had had to pay.

He wanted to wait here until he heard the bells, the church bells ringing people to Mass, before crossing the square and settling his debt to the little saint. But until then he wanted to drink, and he ordered something to drink. He drank. The bells began to ring, summoning people to Mass, and he called, "Waiter, the bill please!" and he paid, got up, went out, and just outside the door he collided with a very tall broad-shouldered man. "Wojtech!" he cried instantly. And the other, just as quickly: "Andreas!" They fell into one another's arms, because they had been miners together in Quebecque, both of them working in the same pit.

"Why don't you wait here till I come back," said Andreas, "I'll be twenty minutes, just as long as Mass takes, not a moment longer!"

"Not a bit of it," said Wojtech. "When did you start going to Mass anyway? If there's anyone I hate more than priests, it's the people who go to them."

"But I'm going to little Thérèse," said Andreas, "I owe her some money."

"Do you mean little St Thérèse?" asked Wojtech.

"Yes, her," replied Andreas.

"How much do you owe her?" asked Wojtech.

"Two hundred francs!" said Andreas.

"In that case I'll go with you!" said Wojtech.

The bells were still ringing. They went into the church and as they stood in the aisle, and Mass was just beginning, Wojtech hissed: "Give me a hundred francs, will you! I've just remembered that there's someone waiting for me outside, otherwise he'll have me put away!"

Andreas immediately handed over both of the hundred-franc notes he had, and said: "I'll see you out there in a minute."

But when it dawned on him that he no longer had the money with which to repay Thérèse, it seemed pointless to him to spend any more time at Mass. Forbearance alone kept him there for another five minutes, then he went back over to the bistro where he found Wojtech waiting for him.

From that moment on, as they assured one another, they were best mates.

In fact, Wojtech didn't have a friend waiting outside, to whom he owed money. He took one of the two hundred-franc notes that Andreas had lent him, and carefully wrapped it in his handkerchief and knotted it up. With the other one, he bought him a drink, and another, and another, and in the evening they went to the house where the obliging girls roosted, and they holed up there for three days, and when they emerged again, it was Tuesday, and Wojtech took leave of Andreas with the words: "Let's meet up again on Sunday, same time, same place."

"See you then!" said Andreas.

"See you!" said Wojtech, and vanished.

14

It was a rainy Tuesday afternoon, and the rain was so heavy that, a moment later, Wojtech had actually vanished. Or at least so it seemed to Andreas. It seemed to him that he had lost his friend in the rain, just as he had chanced to bump into him earlier, and since he only had thirty-five francs left, and

believing himself to be fortune's spoilt darling, and fully confident of further miracles, he decided, like all poor men and
habitual drinkers, to entrust himself to god, to the only god
he believed in. So he went back down the familiar steps, back
down to the Seine, to the home of all the homeless vagrants.

There he bumped into a man who was just about to go up
the steps, and who struck him as familiar. Accordingly,
Andreas greeted him with great politeness. The elderly, spruce
gentleman stopped, looked closely at Andreas and finally
asked: "My dear chap, do you need any money?"

Andreas recognized the voice of the gentleman he had met
three weeks previously in the same place. So he replied: "I
know full well I still owe you money, and I promised to take
it along to St Thérèse. But you see, things kept cropping up. In
fact, I've already made three attempts to pay the money back."

"There must be some mistake," said the elderly, well-dressed
gentleman, "I don't have the honor of your acquaintance. You
must have mistaken me for someone else, but it looks to me as
though you're in a spot of difficulty. Now, you mentioned St
Thérèse, and you must know that I am personally so devoted to
her that I am naturally prepared to advance you whatever sum
you owe her. What is the sum, if you please?"

"Two hundred francs," replied Andreas, "but honestly, you
don't know me! I'm a man of my word, and you'll hardly be
able to send me a bill. I have my honor, but I have no address.
Each night I sleep under one of these bridges."

"Oh, that's all right!" said the gentleman. "That's where I
sleep too. In accepting this money from me, you'll be doing
me a favor for which I shan't be able to thank you enough.
Because I too am so beholden to little Thérèse!"

"In that case," said Andreas, "consider me at your disposal."

He took the money, waited till the gentleman had climbed the steps, and then he climbed up to the quay himself and went directly to the Rue des Quatre Vents, to his old haunt, the Russian-Armenian restaurant Tari-Bari, where he stayed until Saturday night. He then remembered that the following day was Sunday, and that he had an assignation at the church of Sainte Marie des Batignolles.

## 15

The Tari-Bari was crowded, because many clochards would put up there for days, sleeping behind the bar by day, and on the benches at night. Andreas got up very early on Sunday, less to be sure of arriving in time for Mass, than for fear that the landlord would demand payment from him for drink and food and lodging for so many days.

But he miscalculated, because the landlord had got up even earlier than he had. The landlord had known him a long time, and so he knew that our Andreas was inclined to take every opportunity of avoiding paying his bills. And so our Andreas was made to pay, from Tuesday till Sunday, for a lot of food and drink, in fact for rather more than he had personally consumed. For the landlord of the Tari-Bari was able to distinguish between those of his customers who were numerate and those who weren't. And our Andreas, like many drinkers, belonged to the category of the latter. Therefore he paid a great part of the money he had, and then, nothing daunted, set off for the Chapelle de Sainte Marie des Batignolles. He realized, though, that he no longer had enough money to repay Thérèse. But in fact his thoughts were as much on his rendezvous with his friend Wojtech, as on his little creditress.

So he reached the neighborhood of the church, and unfortunately he was once again late for the ten o'clock Mass, and once again people streamed past him out of the church, and when he once again turned aside to go to the bistro, he heard a shout behind him, and felt a rough hand descend on his shoulder. He turned round, and saw that it was a policeman's.

At this our Andreas, who, as we know, had no valid papers, like many of his ilk, was frightened, and he reached into his pocket to give at least the illusion that he might have some valid papers there. But the policeman said: "I know what you're looking for. But you won't find it in your pocket! You've just dropped your wallet. Here it is, and," he added good-naturedly, "remember that's what comes of drinking so many aperitifs so early on a Sunday morning! . . ."

Andreas quickly took the wallet; he barely had the presence of mind to tip his hat to the policeman in gratitude, and swiftly dived into the bistro.

He found Wojtech already there, though it took him a while to recognize him, so that when he finally did so, he greeted him with relief and fervor. Then each man simply wouldn't stop taking it in turn to buy the other a drink, and Wojtech, a polite fellow like the majority of mankind, got up from the bench, gave Andreas pride of place on it, and staggeringly circumnavigated the table and sat down on a chair opposite him, chatting away to him politely. They drank nothing but Pernod.

"Something peculiar happened to me again," said Andreas. "As I'm on my way to our rendezvous, a policeman taps me on the shoulder and says: 'You've lost your wallet.' And he hands me one that doesn't even belong to me, and I take it, and now I want to have a look and see what I've been given."

And he takes out the wallet and looks at it, and there are various bits of paper in it that he doesn't bother about, and he sees there's some money in it too, and he counts the bills, and they come to exactly two hundred francs. And Andreas says: "You see! It's a sign from the Almighty! Now I'm going to go over there and pay my debt at last!"

"That," said Wojtech, "can wait till Mass is over. What do you need Mass for? You can't pay the money back while Mass is going on. Go along to the vestry when it's over, and until then we can sit here and drink!"

"All right," replied Andreas, "whatever you say."

Just at that moment the door opened, and Andreas felt a lightness in his head and a terrible pang in his heart when he saw a girl come in and sit down on the bench directly opposite him. She was very young, younger than any girl he'd ever seen, and she was dressed entirely in sky blue. She was as blue as only the sky can be, and then only on certain blessed days.

So he staggered across to her, bowed and said to the little girl: "What are you doing here?"

"I'm waiting for my parents to come out of Mass; they're meeting me here. Every fourth Sunday," she said, and was quite abashed by the older man who had suddenly come over and started speaking to her. She was a bit afraid of him.

Andreas asked: "What's your name?"

"Thérèse," she said.

"Ah!" cried Andreas, "that's lovely! I never thought that such a great little saint, such a great little creditress would do

me the honor of coming to me after I've failed to go to her
for such a long time."

"I don't understand you," said the little miss, who was
rather bewildered by this.

"That's just your civility," Andreas replied. "That's just your
civility, but I recognize it for what it is. I've owed you two
hundred francs for a long time, and I didn't manage to get to
you and pay them back, holy miss!"

"You don't owe me any money, but I've got some in my
purse—please take it and leave me alone. My parents are
going to be here any minute."

And she gave him a hundred-franc note from her purse.

Wojtech was watching all this in the mirror, and he got up
out of his chair, ordered a couple of Pernods, and was on the
point of dragging Andreas up to the bar to drink them with
him. But just as Andreas gets up to go to the bar, he collaps-
es on the floor like a sack, and everyone in the bistro is
alarmed, including Wojtech, and the little girl most of all. And
because there is no doctor close at hand, and no chemist's
shop, he is dragged across the square to the church, to the
vestry in fact, because even the unbelieving waiters believe
that priests know something about living and dying; and the
girl called Thérèse, she too accompanies them.

So they bring our poor Andreas into the vestry, and unfortunately he's no longer capable of speech, all he can do is to
reach for the left inside pocket of his jacket where he has the
money he owes his little creditress, and he says: "Miss
Thérèse!"—and he sighs once, and he dies.

May God grant us all, all of us drinkers, such a good and
easy death!

*The Legend of the Holy Drinker* is Joseph Roth's last work of fiction, quite deliberately so. Like Andreas's repayment of the two hundred francs, it was his last detail. Again like Andreas, he took his time over it, didn't rush—as most of his books were rushed—but worked at it slowly, with pleasure and pride, for the first four months of 1939. At the end of the fifth, he died. He was not quite forty-five years old.

It is an invidious thing to knock away the props of a dead man, but it is clear that Roth for some time had been running out of reasons to remain alive. Being an exiled writer was attritional, and beyond that, it was perspectiveless. Politically, economically, emotionally and physically he was under threat. Alcoholism had destroyed his health; in 1938 he suffered a heart attack, and he could walk no more than a few steps. He advanced a sophisticated argument that while drink shortened his life in the medium term, in the short term it kept him alive—and he worked hard at testing its logic. After his beloved Hôtel Foyot was pulled down in 1937 (for twelve years it had been "home" to this inveterate and committed hotel-dweller), he moved to the Hôtel de la Poste, above the Café Tournon. His attic room was so tiny that he would fall out of bed straight into the corridor, and thence plunge downstairs into the bar. There he would spend the rest of the day and all night holding court, working, and, increasingly, drinking and brooding beside a small Babel of saucers. His friends and colleagues were dying, often in grotesque circumstances. In 1938, he went to Horváth's funeral, and told friends that the next obituary they would write would be his own. It was the news of another friend's death, the suicide of the playwright Ernst Toller, that precipitated his own collapse, hospitalization and death after four days of bungled treatment.

In the circumstances, it is miraculous that Roth should still have been able to write anything at all, doubly miraculous that it should have come out as light and elegant and sparkling as *The Legend of the Holy Drinker.* The word "legend" is rather soggy in English, but the first dictionary definition of it is "the life of a saint," and Andreas is indeed the unlikeliest of saints. But there are many unlikely saints, and Andreas is as much imbued with hope, faith and charity as the best of them. A merciful irony plays over Andreas—the irony of a loving god who drinks, and who can understand his "hunger," his courtliness, his choice of hostelry, his behavior in the ritzy hotel room. Drink in the book is a philosophy, almost a formal device (as in farce); it is certainly not content, still less milieu. A drinker's blackouts, confusions and carelessness—or liberality—are a way of experiencing the world. The suggestion throughout is, to say it with Robert Frost, "One could do worse."

It is customary—and usually correct—to praise Roth's style for its simplicity. But Roth is not monosyllabic and not Hemingway. He is a thoughtful, quirky and refined writer. Simplicity in English is apt to be taken for rawness, simple-mindedness or blandness, and Roth is very far from being any of these. Nor would he have allowed simplicity to obstruct him in what he was saying. Therefore, after little hesitation, I have decided to plump for a style that gives expression to Roth's ironic capacity, flexibility and qualities of thought. In English, this means using French and Latin words, and this I have very occasionally done, conscious all the time that Roth would have deplored such a practice (and even more the condition of the language that necessitates it), but thinking that in the end he too would have had to adopt it.

Michael Hofmann

November 1988, London